NOTHING ELSE
in 2011

STEVE BEED

Copyright © 2024 Steve Beed

All rights reserved.

ISBN: 9798333580658

DEDICATION

FOR ANNIE, THIS WOULDN'T HAVE HAPPENED WITHOUT YOU, AND TO MARTIN, STEVE AND DAVE FOR YOUR HELP AND ENCOURAGEMENT

Acknowledgements

This book is a work of fiction, all characters and events are make believe.

CONTENTS

CHAPTER 1   BEACH
CHAPTER 2   CENTRE
CHAPTER 3   PROBLEM
CHAPTER 4   JOB
CHAPTER 5   ARRIVAL
CHAPTER 6   TALK
CHAPTER 7   STORY
CHAPTER 8   WALK
CHAPTER 9   ESCAPE
CHAPTER 10 FARM
CHAPTER 11 WAKE-UP CALL
CHAPTER 12 CAFÉ
CHAPTER 13 ANOTHER HOUSE
CHAPTER 14 WAIT
CHAPTER 15 STRANGER
CHAPTER 16 MEETING
CHAPTER 17 NIGHT
CHAPTER 18 RETURN
CHAPTER 19 HOMECOMING
CHAPTER 20 REUNION
CHAPTER 21 GRADUATION
CHAPTER 22 POSTSCRIPT

CHAPTER 1
Beach

It is the end of summer – thank goodness!

It's not that I don't like the summer, I like it very much. I certainly don't mind having five weeks off work, who wouldn't? It's just that this summer nothing went as planned, it was awful and I am happy to be going back to work again.

Before August arrived I had been looking forward to a holiday in Corfu with Nicole, my now ex-girlfriend. It was supposed to be sunshine, meals out, days by the pool and nights of sex. A chance to relax and spend some quality time together, at least that was the plan when we booked it on a snowy January afternoon. As you have probably guessed by now, the holiday didn't happen like that. The week before we were due to leave, with the packing half done, we had a disagreement - that turned into an argument - that turned into the terminal throes of what had been a bumpy relationship at the best of times.

I'm not saying I was blameless; I may have said some unpleasant things in the heat of the moment. I don't remember precisely what, you would probably have to ask Nicole – or my next-door-neighbour. Anyway, she had wanted to get a tattoo before we went away, fair enough, it's her skin. I turned down the suggestion that I should get a matching green lizard on my own shoulder and she threw a hissy fit. Apparently, this showed that I 'lacked commitment to the relationship.' So really, who needs that kind of shit?

Anyway, I was left with a bought and paid for holiday for two that it was way too late to cancel. I considered just writing it off and cutting my losses, but at the eleventh hour I changed my mind, repacked my bag and went by myself. Who knew, I might even meet someone nice - a holiday fling type of thing. Yeah right! First, I had the joy of questions, answers and cavity searches with grim-faced customs officials. Then I found myself surrounded by young families trailing around with their kids – all liberally coated with ice-cream and sun lotion. There were also a large number of drunk, lovesick teenagers - and Germans. Mostly Germans.

The holiday was so tedious I ended up being persuaded to sign on for every trip available with Tracey, the extraordinarily cheerful and smiley holiday rep. Most of the trips were to see piles of old stones in various configurations, largely unrecognisable as the places they were purporting to have been. I also took part in an early morning bird watchers special. This is not an activity I have ever taken an interest in before, but I thought it might be interesting or fun. It turned out it was neither. Up at four thirty, standing in bushes by the side of parched fields, while people around me pointed, whispered and made notes in their special bird watching notebooks. The combination of dust and pollen resulted in me having several sneezing outbursts, which is apparently not a done thing when you are trying to catch sight of shy and timid creatures. The bus ride back to the hotel was awkward to say the least.

I ate alone and drank too much – also alone, although there was one night out with a very pleasant and outgoing woman called Mel from Manchester. I managed to blow any possibility of that going anywhere by dominating the conversation with my list of complaints about Nicole's many shortcomings and how awful our relationship had been. I got through the fortnight, but was looking forward to getting home again by the end of the two weeks.

I returned to the news that Dad had broken his wrist falling from a ladder. I don't know why he was up the ladder, at his age shouldn't he be taking it easy? I asked him, but he was evasive. When I saw him with the plaster cast on his arm I realised, in an overdue epiphany, that maybe Dad wasn't my invincible childhood hero anymore. It occurred to me, maybe for the first time, that my parents were starting to look like old people. Which is to say, the same as they had always looked, but older. I shouldn't have been surprised, they are both retired and in their late sixties, but I had never seen him hurt like this before. I looked at how grey both my parent's hair had become, their lined faces and the imperceptibly slower more careful movements that belong to older people, like my grandparents. Again, I shouldn't have been surprised; they are grandparents themselves, several times over - courtesy of both my brother and sister. Nevertheless, it still caught me by surprise.

Long story short, I spent the rest of my holiday helping Dad with jobs that required two hands. I swear he had me doing jobs that he had been putting off for years, waiting for this precise moment; resetting patio slabs, digging out tree roots, getting blisters – all under his direct and detailed supervision. The upside was endless cups of tea and plenty of home cooking while my mum kept reiterating what a 'good lad' I was.

After I came home from Greece Nicole messaged me regularly, wanting to 'talk about it' - she thought she may have made a mistake; I don't, although I did finally cave in and agree to meet her. That was definitely a mistake, she came to my flat, drank too much and wouldn't leave. There were lots of histrionics and tears and at times I nearly weakened – but I kept my resolve. Like all my previous relationships, this wasn't right for me. Nicole had been absolutely correct about one thing, the bit about lacking commitment. I don't have a good track record with sustaining meaningful relationships. The evening left me unsettled and thoughtful for several days, taking stock of what I was doing with my life. My friends were all married – some more than once – with rapidly growing families, while I drifted through a seemingly endless stream of doomed affairs.

So now that I am back at work, I'm glad to be busy and back into my routine. Instead of being at the beck and call of my now-recovered dad, adrift in the timeless sea of holiday, my days are once again punctuated by regular time-checks, subdivided into precise segments with predictable fixed routines. After 25 years – a quarter of a century! – I am comfortable with letting my days and weeks be guided by my calendar, diary, watch and a timetable.

It also means I have dropped back into habits that had become erratic in the busy-ness of summer. My evening walk on the beach is one of these.

Come home, change from a shirt and tie to jeans and a tee-shirt, then walk from my flat to the end of the road, where I arrive at the beach. Habit dictates that I then walk the mile and a bit to the cliffs, before returning home and making tea, marking books and watching crap on the TV. Only the harshest weather, a date, or a visit to my parents, causes a break in this ritual. Although even those things could usually be worked around to fit in a short stroll.

This evening it is warm, the sun is still doing its best for the time of year. Although summer is now behind me there is no need for a coat, I have tied my jumper around my waist and have been joined by a host of others enjoying a Friday evening walk. Dog walkers, whose excited hounds chase tennis balls or drag along pieces of driftwood. Families making the most of this mini summer revival, with welly-booted children squealing as they splash in and out of the pools left by the retreating tide.

I am lost in a reverie of my own thoughts, rewinding the day, planning the evening, and thinking about what to fill my time with over the coming weekend. As I approach my turning point, I vaguely register that someone is sitting on the rocks under the cliff. I don't pay that much attention – it is a popular spot to stop before making the return journey back down the beach.

The figure is silhouetted against the jagged red cliffs, sandwiched between the dirty yellow sand and the fading blue sky. Gulls are wheeling lazily, watching to see what gets left behind by the waves that wash lethargically along the shore. It is a beautiful evening; I had thought I would sit on the rocks myself for a while when I arrived, as is often my habit. I hope the person currently occupying 'my' boulder will have decided to move on by the time I get there. I can see, now that I am getting closer, it is a woman in a blue coat. She is showing no signs of moving; she is just sitting – apparently enjoying the afternoon too. I will have to select an alternative perch, or just turn around and walk back, if she doesn't go in the next minute or two.

She doesn't go. She stays where she is and appears to be watching me as I close the distance. I think it is probably my egocentric imagination (or paranoia) doing its thing, but as I approach she raises her hand and waves.

I look behind me, there is no-one else close to me, here at the quiet end of the beach. I squint and peer, trying to make out who it is. I'm sure I would recognise her by now if it was someone I knew well, perhaps she has mistaken me for someone else.

I am now closing the gap between us rapidly; I can see that she is smiling expectantly. Her coat looks better suited to an office than the beach. Her silvery blonde hair is untied and drops onto her shoulders, she is wearing grey trousers and smart shoes – again, not beach attire. I'm not good at this sort of thing, but I would guess she is in her 50s. Now I can see her face more clearly, she is definitely watching me as I approach and seems pleased to see me. I still don't recognise her though.

I'm only a couple of steps away. I am about to speak, a tentative greeting. At the same time I am frantically scouring my memory banks, desperately trying to find a name to go with the face of the woman who clearly seems to know who I am. She does not appear to be planning to say anything; she merely waits expectantly with a smile on her face, apparently confident that I will make the connection if she gives me enough time.

I think of a face - shorter and yellower hair, no glasses, younger - and something flickers on the edge of my memory, then suddenly everything clicks into place, I stop dead in my own sandy footprints.

"Julia?"

"Actually, it's Alice, that's my real name. Hello and nice to see you too. It's been a long time."

I just stand and stare, I have no idea what to say. My brain is still busy trying to make sense of Julia's – or Alice's – reappearance after more than 20 years. Julia/Alice had been part of a secretive government department, I never found out which, that had intervened when I did something stupid at college. It had been a difficult time that I have tried hard not to think about in the intervening years. Now it all comes flooding back.

Have I done something wrong? Was it the trip to Greece? Has something else happened? Am I in trouble? A part of my psyche is suddenly a scared 20-year-old again, I manage to stutter, "Hi."

"Well, don't just stand there, come and share my rock."

I just stand there.

"What do you want?"

"Just a chat, but I'd be more comfortable if we were both sitting."

"Am I in trouble?"

"No, come and sit down."

I finally take the last few steps to the rock and sit near – but not too near – Julia. Alice. It's Alice now. I am having trouble adjusting, she was always Julia to me, and even though I had always known this was probably not her real name, it's difficult. Maybe Alice isn't really her name either. The last time I had seen her was in a pub in 1987, I thought that had been the end of it. The fact I had continued to get a Christmas card every December, always with a short perfunctory message written in the same shade of blue ink, should have warned me it wasn't. I had been assuming it was just a glitch in the system, that I was still on a list that had never been updated. I guess I was wrong.

"Are you okay?" she asks.

"Yeah, I suppose."

"You look like you've seen a ghost."

This was accompanied by a tiny smile at the corners of Alice's mouth. I allowed myself the slightest of smiles in return then repeat, "What do you want?"

"Like I said, just to talk."

"Why? Why now?"

"Well, it's complicated, but I need to ask you a favour. It's a one-time deal and a chance to wipe the slate clean."

"I kind of thought it already was, after all this time."

"No, officially you're still a 'person of interest', do you think everybody spends that long in security at airports, or gets seen at the doctors so quickly, or gets enough tax rebates to keep them comfortable and solvent?"

"I never really thought about it." It's true, it had never really occurred to me that anybody else had the same experiences as me, why would it? Now she has said it out loud I have to confront it, and it kind of makes sense. I felt a brief flicker of anger that they had been intruding for so long, "So you've been watching me all this time? 25 years?"

"Well, somebody has, just checking in every so often really. It's so much easier now we've all got these."

She pulls her hand from her pocket to show she is holding her mobile. I automatically reach and put my hand over the pocket where my own phone is safely stored.

"You hacked my phone?"

"Not exactly, it's our phone. We set it up so we could keep tabs on you if we needed to. It's how I knew you'd be here."

"But..." I remember now that the phone had been sent to me unsolicited a couple of years ago, as an incentive for me to sign up with a provider, the anger flashes back again, "...shit! Seriously!"

"You signed the waiver."

"But....oh, the small print."

"You'd be surprised how many people don't bother to read it. Or maybe you wouldn't. Anyway, it's beside the point, can you do us a favour? Or at least give it some consideration? It's your decision in the end."

I'm hesitant; it's hard to agree to something when you don't know what it is. I'm also still slightly stunned to find out that Julia – who isn't Julia (although I'd always suspected as much) had been watching me all this time. Maybe I should have expected it, but I've been busy getting on with my life, with the nitty gritty of eat, work, sleep, play. The whole sorry episode had slowly moved to the back recesses of my mind – not forgotten, but not relevant to the here and now. Except right now it is suddenly relevant again. "What is it you need me to do?"

"It's complicated, I'll explain everything tomorrow, if you are willing to give it a go."

"Well give me a clue."

"I don't think this is a good place for a private talk, do you? You never know who's listening." Again, a tiny smile, and this time I'm sure she winks as I look sideways at her. She actually fucking winks. I blush as I recall the secret plans I had hatched with Grace sitting on this very rock - with Alice/Julia, or someone, listening to every word, and me thinking I was being so careful and cunning. I've decided, "Okay, where are we meeting?"

"Go home, pack an overnight bag and a car will pick you up at 7, I'll see you tomorrow. And thanks, I really mean it, I wouldn't ask if it wasn't important."

"Why? Where will..." I start to ask. But Alice is already up and walking to the road that runs alongside the beach, where a blue Ford Focus is waiting. Her heels sink into the sand with every step, but she keeps a steady pace unimpeded by her inappropriate attire. I think about running after her with my questions, but decide it would be pointless. I stay on the rock for a moment, wondering what I have let myself in for, not that I felt I really had a choice. I watch the car pick up speed and get smaller as it leaves me on the sand with my questions, then I start the long walk back, with a hundred questions and no answers rattling around in my head. The anger has been replaced with weary resignation, as if I had known all along that this was how it was going to be.

At home I check the kitchen clock – 5.45. I still have plenty of time to grab something to eat, a ready meal from the fridge. The microwave starts its countdown as I lean on the kitchen counter and run through everything that just happened,

'What kind of favour?'

'Why do I need to pack a bag?'

'Where am I going?'

'Why did I agree?'

'What happens if I say no?'

'What the fuck is going on?'

As things stand, I had nothing much planned this weekend, so there is nothing to cancel. I wonder if I should call anyone and let them know I'm going, but I'm not sure how long I will be gone. Or, for that matter, how I would explain it. I don't really want to start fabricating tales that will fall apart under any kind of scrutiny and decide to leave it for now.

Once I have eaten and the kitchen is tidied, I retrieve my bag from the bottom of the wardrobe and start filling it with a random selection of underwear, socks, t-shirts and a wash bag. I also put in my MP3 player and my copy of Margaret Atwood's 'The Year of the Flood', which is half-read on my bedside table. Purchased after waiting for the sequel to Oryx and Crake for nearly five years, I had been hoping to finish it this weekend.

All of this happens while the stereo plays '30 Something' at a volume that is loud enough to distract me, but not loud enough to piss off the neighbours. Although how Carter USM could annoy anyone is a mystery to me. I sing along loudly.

Before I know where the time has gone it is nearly seven. I look out of the window and see a blue car, the same one that Julia –Alice, Alice, Alice! – got into earlier I'm sure. I hook my bag over my shoulder, then take a deep breath. Patting myself down to make sure I have everything I let myself out, locking the door behind me.

Alice

The helicopter dropped gently to the ground and Alice disembarked, ducking as she walked briskly towards the squat building. Before she was even half way there the black helicopter rose noisily back into the air, making her hair and coat flap about her as she completed the short journey.

Mrs Baker was waiting by the door – of course. Alice had long since ceased to wonder what Mrs Baker did when she wasn't working. She had no relations that anybody at the centre knew of (she could find out if she really wanted, but it was generally considered bad form to look into colleagues in your own centre) and very rarely left the site. She liked being busy and treated the staff and transient visitors as her surrogate family. In her 70's now she showed no signs of slowing down, Alice had tried to talk to her on more than one occasion about her retirement plans, but had been given short shrift each time. Another problem for another day.

"Everything is on schedule, the report is on your desk," Mrs Baker half-shouted over the sound of the retreating helicopter.

"Thank you, is the room all ready?"

"I saw to it myself. There's coffee in your office."

"Thanks."

"You're welcome."

This brief conversation took place as Alice entered the building, and was mostly superfluous. Alice had already received and read the report she needed, confirming the pick-up, and she had no doubts that the room would be ready. Likewise, she knew there would be fresh coffee, there always was. Still, Mrs Baker (Alice had never found out what happened to Mr Baker) was the old school type of administrator that liked to tell you things personally. Alice didn't mind this, in fact she found it reassuring to know that someone was keeping tabs on things apart from her.

It had taken some time to reach this level of familiarity; her relationship with Mrs Baker had been frosty when Alice first met her. Most of the progress had been made since she returned to the centre full time, to fill O'Brien's retiring shoes. He had specifically asked her to take over, and after years of itinerant globe-trotting with the foreign office, she was glad to have a base to work from again.

She went to her office and poured herself some coffee, which was as fresh as had been promised, then sat at her desk. She paused and looked at the folders lined up in front of her, all relating to a single issue. She wondered again if she was doing the right thing. Part of her thought she should let sleeping dogs lie. But another part, more pragmatic and incisive, had seen how this could work - as long as the sleeping dog agreed to play his part.

In a sense it was all academic right now anyway. The wheels had been set in motion and the cogs had begun to turn, for better or for worse. She logged onto her computer and reread the files, updating notes and observations. A notification appeared in the corner of her screen; an update from Carl.

She had worked with Carl for a number of years now, he was one of her best operatives. She had plucked him from the services when he ran into a spot of bother that had threatened to derail his career. A senior colleague, an old friend from her foreign office days, with a finger in a lot of pies, had recommended him to her personally. He was good at what he did, his slightly maverick nature fitted the work well. They needed people who could follow orders, but also act independently and make their own decisions when necessary and Carl fitted that skillset.

When he came to her attention, he had been detained by the military police for assaulting a senior officer in Afghanistan and was facing a court martial. Her colleague acknowledged that questions should be asked, particularly when someone has had an arm, their nose and jaw broken – but he didn't think the right questions were being asked.

The girl who had been at the centre of the incident was slight, probably only a teenager, scared and bleeding. Maybe she reminded him of someone, or maybe it was her tears and the pleading look in her fear-filled hazel eyes that had been enough to make him act the way he did; but more likely it was because the idiot, drunken assailant who was standing over the girl had invited him to join in if he wanted – he didn't.

Alice had asked the right questions when she met him, then made the problem go away, in return Carl had agreed to join her team. To be honest, she would have tried to make the charges go away even if he had not, because he had been protecting a young girl from a grown man, and nobody likes a bully. He was reliable and hard-working, and, unusually for someone from the services, preferred to work alone.

*

Carl remembers this as a turning point in his life too. After a night out, he had come across a girl being knocked around by a man twice her size, softening her up before dragging her into a doorway and assaulting her further. He had seen red and a flurry of well-aimed kicks and punches, delivered as he had been trained, resolved the situation. He had stopped himself from doing further harm to the man, but had still ended up in Colchester with an uncertain future ahead of him.

When he had come to the girl's aid, he had no idea who the assailant was aside from a white male. It turned out to be a senior ranking officer from a different battalion. He knew he was facing, at best, a dishonourable discharge and an uncertain future when Alice had appeared in his cell. She had spent some time talking with him, then made an offer that he really couldn't refuse. He found himself saved from disgrace and moving into a new job that suited him better than the work he had originally signed up for.

He had been unshakeably loyal to Alice ever since. It helped that he had enormous respect for her judgement and the way she ran her operation. They were so often on the same wavelength that he could second guess what she wanted him to do a lot of the time, although she usually seemed to be comfortably two steps ahead of him.

His report was succinct, it merely informed her that he was en-route with his passenger, that everything had gone smoothly and that they would be arriving at the expected time. What was less succinct and informal was the addendum that he had added. He often did this, knowing that it would not form part of any official transcripts, should they ever be needed.

'He seems scared to death, what have you told him is going to happen? Whatever it was, can you tell him it will definitely occur if he doesn't stop fucking about with the radio?'

Alice laughed and shook her head, then deleted the final part of the message before archiving the rest. Good, he was safely on his way.

CHAPTER 2
Centre

The countryside is flashing by as I try to get myself comfortable in the passenger seat of the Focus. We are long past any familiar landmarks or name places, having driven for several hours. At first I had been hesitant to get into the car, the driver assured me it was alright, "It's okay, I've been told to do whatever you ask. Anytime you want to stop, turn around or even just get out and walk off, just say the word."

His smart casual dress, a black polo shirt over broad shoulders, and short haircut, hint at a military background; a Bear Grylls look. His reassuring smile somehow gave me confidence that he would be following his orders to the letter.

"Where are we going?"

"I'm afraid I'm not allowed to tell you that, you'll see when we get there."

Of course, I realise now that I won't see anything at all. It's already getting dark outside, and if we don't arrive shortly it will be full dark by the time we reach our final destination. Also, as stated previously, I already have no idea where we currently are.

I have ascertained that the driver is called Carl, Alice is his boss, he doesn't really like this car, but it does what it's supposed to do. His own car is an Audi which he treated himself to last year. He hadn't brought along any decent CDs for the journey. He seems like a nice enough guy, but the majority of my questions are met with the same answer, "I'm afraid I can't tell you that."

It is limiting the conversation somewhat. I switch the radio back on, the earlier offerings of Katy Perry, Adele and Oly Murs on sad rotation had become too much. Now Annie Mac had been replaced by Westwood, Christ that man has awful taste in music – and why does he talk like that? I miss John Peel.

I switch it off again and look at the passing lights of cars, shops, houses and pubs as they parade past and disappear into the night. Closing my eyes I lean back into the seat and let myself get hypnotised by the ambient sounds of the car in motion, eventually falling into a light sleep. It's the kind of sleep that you half-wake from occasionally, never quite sure if you are in the car or just in a dream about being in car.

I wake fully again to find us travelling through pitch blackness; the only lights are the gently illuminating glow from the dashboard dials and a small patch of light that races ahead of us. At the edges of this pool of light is scrubby grass, bleached white by the ferocity of the headlights.

"Where are we?" I attempt to stretch in the confined space.

"Nearly there."

I sigh in response to this non-answer, slump back into the seat and stare into the darkness. We round an invisible bend and I see a row of lights in the distance, they gradually grow as we draw closer and I can begin to make out a low grey building, a fence and a gatehouse. Although I have never seen it from this perspective before I get a sick feeling of recognition, there are enough clues for me to realise that I have been here before.

"Stop."

Carl obligingly slows the car and comes to a halt.

"We're just about there now."

"I know, I just need to see."

I open the door and climb out to stand by the side of the road while Carl waits patiently in the car with the engine idling. Even in the darkness I can make out the empty heathland all around me. I look at the building, surrounded by its halo of lights. It is squat and utilitarian, trying unsuccessfully to look as inconspicuous as possible. We are indeed almost there, close enough for me to see the person in the gatehouse step outside and peer in our direction across the windswept tarmac, ghostly white in our headlights. I take a deep breath then get back into the car which moves forward again.

The gatekeeper lets us through when he recognises both the car and driver and we pull into a well-tended gravel car park with a sparse smattering of vehicles. Carl leads me the short distance to the entrance, along a floodlit path under the starry sky. Julia – no, not Julia, Alice - is waiting and smiles as I approach. I smile back, but the smile is only on my face.

"How was your journey?"

"Long. Where are we?"

"The north."

I had already guessed that, if we had been travelling south we would have been in France, or the English Channel, long ago. I stop outside the doors.

"Am I going to be locked in?"

"No, you can leave whenever you want, just ask. Now come in and have a drink, I bet Carl didn't stop and get one on the way did he?"

He had actually, but that doesn't mean I don't want another now. I follow Alice as Carl goes back towards the gatehouse on some errand or mission.

"Goodnight, see you tomorrow," he says as leaves.

"Okay, finish your paperwork in the morning, it's not urgent unless you have anything to add to it."

"Okay ma'am, see you at briefing."

Alice takes me to a small windowless room. It is perfunctory, like a bad hotel room, with a bed, desk, chair and shower cubicle. It is the same as the room I remember from my last time here, although I am relieved to see there are handles on both sides of the door this time. A smartly dressed older lady catches up with us and places a cup of tea on the desk; I am certain that I recognise her from my last visit. I had caught glimpses of her as I was escorted around the centre, although she must be as old as the hills now. Mind you, we were all younger then of course. I thank her and she takes her leave.

"So, why am I here?"

"I think we should talk in the morning, let's get some sleep first shall we?"

"No clues then? After dragging me all this way."

"Only that I'm sure you'll want to help when I explain everything. Use the intercom if you need anything, there are staff on all night," she points to the panel on the wall. "I'll see you in the morning. And believe it or not, it is nice to see you again, I'm glad you agreed to come."

I'm not so sure that I had a choice, even though Alice seems reassured to think that I did.

"I wish it wasn't here."

"I'm sorry, that's just how it is. It shouldn't be for long, see you in the morning."

"Yeah, goodnight."

I unpack my meagre belongings as I drink my tea. The first thing I realise is that I omitted to put my pyjamas in, I idly wonder what would happen if I used the intercom to ask for some, then opt instead to sleep in my tee shirt and boxers. I don't think I'm tired, being here has opened a Pandora's Box of unwelcome and unwanted memories that make me sure I'll spend the rest of the evening tossing restlessly as I battle with my demons from yesteryear.

In spite of my misgivings, the lateness of the hour and the length of the day take their toll. I drift into a deep sleep after putting in my earphones and choosing a selection of slightly ethereal and calming 10,000 Maniacs tracks as my chosen band to wind down with at the end this unexpectedly long day.

Alice

Alice sighs. She is back at her desk and is unable to sleep even though there is nothing productive she can do right now. On her computer monitor are two boxes, each showing a grainy infra-red image of a sleeping figure. One tosses and turns restlessly, frequently getting up and pacing around the tiny room. The other is sprawled across the bed snoring, looking like he doesn't have a care in the world.

Maybe he didn't before yesterday she thought. She had agonised over whether this was the right thing to do, she hadn't seen him for 24 years and hadn't really expected to ever need to make contact with him again. But for a confluence of circumstances, coincidences and fate she wouldn't have. Now she was following her gut feeling that he was right for this, the person they needed. If all went well, she hoped he would be useful to her, along the way he might get some of the closure that had been so elusive for him all those years ago. God knows he deserves it.

The second restless sleeper is slight, covered by the blanket that she held over herself as she wriggled and twisted. The youngest resident at the centre for decades, her arrival had been uneventful, no questions, no rancour, no insisting on making a phone call or having a lawyer. She had merely seemed stunned, overwhelmed by what had happened and unable to make sense of it.

Alice sipped her coffee, realised it was now cold and put it to one side, inwardly lamenting the fact that it would be several hours before fresh coffee was initiated by Mrs Baker. She checked her messages, one from Carl, which she had expected.

'*Off to collect next package.*'

She had wondered if he might take a rest period first. Evidently not, he was keen to be in the right place good and early for tomorrow. Also, he wasn't really a resting type of person. Alice was, she retreated to her bunk in a small room off of her office.

The centre is quiet, but it doesn't sleep. It hums away to itself as it circulates second-hand air, the semi-silence punctuated by occasional muffled sounds of closing doors and footsteps. It goes about it's unknown and unknowable business. Electronic eyes send a constant stream of images to a room banked with CCTV monitors, where a man known only as Bob sits looking at the largely unchanging pictures that flicker in front of him throughout the night. In a sub-level, deep under the ground, computers monitor the unseen world beyond the centre with their electronic tentacles. The gatekeeper looks across the barren, starlit moorland and the thin strip of tarmac that connects them with the outside world.

CHAPTER 3
Problem

A light rap on my door wakes me up. I am momentarily disorientated as I emerge from unremembered dreams, then abruptly wide awake as the door opens and Alice comes in with two mugs of tea. She puts one on the desk and pulls the chair out with her free hand.

"Cup of tea?" she asks as she sits down.

"Er, yeah, what time is it?"

"Nearly eight, sorry to wake you. I wanted to make sure we got going early this morning, that way you've still got plenty of time to get back home if that's what you decide to do."

Alice is momentarily Julia again, sitting across the room from me in a white blouse and tight-fitting trousers in this timeless room with the underlying smell of cleaning fluids. The memories of feelings – anticipation, fear, uncertainty, along with the not knowing what is happening or why I am here - all crowd in. For the first time in years, I feel like I really need a cigarette. I rally around.

"Not a problem, I'm usually up about now anyway." This is not entirely true, I'm hardly ever up before 9 on a Saturday. I quietly wonder if Alice knows that this is not true, if she does, she doesn't let on, we are both keeping up our ends of the social contract - pretending that my private life is now, or ever has been, private.

"So, why am I here?"

"There's breakfast in the meeting room, second door on the left when you're dressed. When you're up I'll explain everything, then you can choose whether to stay or not."

I watch Alice carefully put the chair back by the desk. As soon as she leaves, I hurry to the loo then recycle yesterday's clothes and follow the directions I have been given to find food. Alice is waiting for me, the room is one I have been in before, many years ago. Then it was furnished with nothing but tables and chairs; now it has a large whiteboard on the far wall, a laptop sits on the table and there is a heated trolley next to a small table with plates and cutlery in one corner. It is more of a conference space than the interrogation room it had been on my last visit. Alice is sitting looking at a computer screen but looks up and acknowledges me when I enter the room.

"Help yourself from the trolley," Alice indicates the corner where it is positioned and I go over and help myself from the offerings as instructed – it would be rude not to, food is food. I take it to the table and sit across from Alice while I eat and she drinks coffee.

"Feel better with some food in you?" she asks.

"Much, although I'd feel better still if I knew why I was here."

"I know, thanks for your patience, I'll get to the point."

She presses a key on her computer and the whiteboard flashes into life. It is a video of what is clearly one of the rooms here at the centre, tidier than the one I stayed in previously but clearly recognisable. A figure is sitting on the bed with their head in their hands, a young female with a riot of curly hair. She looks up and I can see her face clearly, my world drops away from beneath me – a shift in reality causing me to momentarily forget to breathe. Grace? I glance at Alice and then look back at the screen. There is a timestamp in the bottom corner of the screen and I see that this is a live feed, my brain tries to work out what is going on while Alice waits patiently. Eventually the cogs turn in my brain and I manage to make sense of what I'm looking at.

"Is that…?"

"Yes, it's Sydney."

I haven't seen Grace's daughter since she was 9 or 10, a rumbunctious bundle of energy who made me play every board game she owned over the course of a weekend – Hungry Hippos and Connect Four anyone? Communication with Grace has tailed off in recent years, now only Christmas greetings and very occasional, perfunctory, messages as the immediacy of daily life has taken precedence for both of us. I feel a pang of guilt, even though I know it wasn't just me that didn't keep in touch. I can't get over how much Syd looks like my 20-year-old memory of Grace.

"Why's she here?"

"The same reason anybody ends up here. She's in trouble."

"What kind of trouble?"

"Ah, Catch 22, I can't tell you unless you're in. Sorry, I'm not trying to pressure you."

She may not be trying to pressure me, but I feel myself tensing up. So far I have managed to act as if there is some element of this which is normal, but it's not. I am dizzy with memories from a quarter of a century ago, things I thought I had let go of, things that I had moved on from. Now I feel like that scared 20-year-old again, helpless and trapped.

"I need some fresh air, and I need a cigarette. And yes, I am aware of the contradiction in that statement."

"No problem, just head out front, I'll join you there in a moment."

"I can just walk out?"

"Yes, you can come and go as you please."

I sense that this may not be entirely true, nevertheless I take one more look at Syd, sitting on her bed, and walk the short distance to the main door, which swooshes open as I approach it. I step outside into the cool air of a stiff breeze. I consider going back in to collect a sweatshirt, then decide I'd prefer to suffer the cold for a few minutes than to go back inside the building. The bleak moorland undulates and rolls into the distance like a purple carpet. There are no other buildings visible in any direction, the only mark on the landscape is the single strip of tarmac that leads away from the gate. Checking my phone I find no new messages other than the multiple unanswered ones from Nicole from the previous week and I have no intention of reading them, let alone responding. There is no more signal here than there was inside the building. I don't know if I am out of range or if it is blocked, whatever, it's the same difference either way.

I hear the doors slide open behind me and footsteps approaching. I don't turn and look, I just assume it is Alice joining me, I am right.

"Please don't take any photos, it's strictly not allowed."

I look at the phone still in my hand, it figures, I slide it back into my pocket.

"I'm not really sure what I'd take photos of, there's nothing here."

"I think it's rather beautiful, I like to watch the clouds by following their shadows across the moor."

I look, she's right, it is quite mesmeric. Once you have seen the dark pools oozing over the uneven ground you can't unsee them. I let my gaze rise to the clouds themselves, something jars but I can't put my finger on what it is. Alice holds out a packet of cigarettes and a lighter.

"Are you sure?"

"I'm sure."

I'm not. I know it's stupid and I don't need it, I've been stopped for so long. But actually I think I do need it, the last 12 hours have bought a host of, mostly unwelcome, memories flooding back. Memories of a time I had not forgotten, but had managed to put away in a closed memory box. Occasionally there would be a name or an image that would open that box the tiniest bit and things would seep out. But now the lid had been thrown wide open and the whole lot had been emptied out, buzzing through my mind and reigniting the chain of events that had started with me, Sarah, Lisa, Stewart and

Jo finding the cylinder we weren't meant to while on a drunken night out. It had led to Lisa's death and a chain reaction of events that had left me with a life full of recriminations and fear of repercussions. It still felt raw, and thinking of Lisa in particular was painful, wondering what her life would have been like. Would she have changed the world? Raised children? I'm sure she could have done anything she had set her mind to and it seems unnecessarily cruel that she had been the one who died and not me.

I open the packet and put a cigarette in my mouth. Even after all this time the action feels natural, part of my brain is already trembling with anticipation, the mental equivalent of a watering mouth. It is all I can do to fiddle the cigarette back into its packet and bury them deep in my pocket. Suddenly I realise what had been unsettling before, "There's no lines."

"Eh?"

"In the sky, vapour trails or whatever they're called. It's like when that volcano in Iceland erupted last year, no planes."

"Oh, I see. No, no planes here, it's a no-fly zone."

I wonder what I would see if I looked at this location on Google maps, I suspect it would show me a beautiful expanse of empty moorland, maybe a caption in Gothic script saying 'here be dragons' with a skull and crossbones.

I come to a decision, I feel like I have already been skilfully maneuvered into a corner anyway, "Okay, I'm in. What do you want me to do?"

"Thank you, I knew I could rely on you. Come inside and I'll explain."

I take one last breath of clear, unfiltered air and turn back towards the door, following Alice inside. I can't resist glancing at her buttocks, she still looks good. Funny how she had seemed so much older than me before, now it feels like I've caught up. A different time or place and I might have asked her out for a drink. I'm pretty sure I would know her answer, but you have to try sometimes don't you?

Syd

She sits on the edge of bed, alert, listening, waiting. At the moment she doesn't know where she is or why she's here. She has been alternately twirling her fingers into her hair then chewing on her nails. Everything is silent apart from the distant hum of the air-conditioning and occasional muffled, far-off sounds. She had unsuccessfully tried to open the handle-less door but could not bring herself to press the intercom button, unsure of what she would say or what the response would be. Somebody had brought her toast and tea earlier, it remained untouched on the tiny desk. There are rules and laws about this sort of thing, she knows they can't just keep her here, locked up for no reason. She is biding her time, ready to confront them with this.

When they appeared at her flat yesterday, with their military-looking uniforms and blacked out van, she had been too surprised to object or resist their requests for her to come quietly. Everything had been so quick, from the moment the front door swung open and she went to see if it was Rick coming back, to the time she was being helped up into the back of the van, can't have been more than a couple of minutes. Now she has had time to think about it she can't even recall any of their names or what reason they had given for requiring her to accompany them – she was not even certain that any of that information had been offered. Everything seemed a little surreal in retrospect, and she was cross with herself for not having had the sense to ask for a phone call or a lawyer. Not that she knew any lawyers, but she knew it was the sort of thing that was supposed to happen.

And where was Rick? He hadn't been around for a couple of days now. He was always full of froth and noise about peoples' rights and the inequality and unfairness of life. He would have known what to do, although thinking about it she wouldn't be surprised if this was something to do with him. He could be a bloody idiot sometimes; like the night he took her out to spray paint the single word 'occupy' on every blank wall and advertising board in the area – until a passing police car freaked her out and she insisted that they went home. Or the time he turned up at her Wednesday afternoon rounders game in the park with an airhorn which he blasted loudly as he cheered and whistled every time her team had done something remotely advantageous. Standing far enough away from them to be distant, but close enough to be annoying. It was funny at first, then irritating until, finally, the other players made her go and plead with him to stop.

She was beginning to wonder what it was that she had seen in him, aside from the raw physical attraction. She supposed it had been fun at times, but he was so opinionated and serious a lot of the time and didn't seem to have much interest in what she said or thought. Still, nothing she could do about any of that now, except dwell on it in all this unexpected free time.

Against her expectations she found herself wanting to call her mum. It didn't seem a very adult wish to her, but then sometimes being an adult wasn't easy. She was finding that out now and wished she had spent more time with Mum when she last went home, instead of shutting herself in her room when she wasn't out drinking with her friends.

She crossed the room and took a sip of tea, it was lukewarm, just cool enough to wash down a few mouthfuls of cold toast. She sat back on the bed and waited, watching the door and picking at the skin at the edges of her fingernails.

CHAPTER 4
Job

I go back to the meeting room, following Alice. The breakfast things have all been taken away. The drinks remain and I help myself to a fresh mug of tea while Alice pours herself some coffee, then we return to the table.
"So, what do you need me to do? What have I signed up for?"

"It's complicated, where shall I start?"

The question is clearly rhetorical, Alice knows exactly where to start. She seems to have this planned, plotted and prepared, seemed fairly certain I would be part of whatever it was when she showed me the video feed earlier. I humour her anyway and ask a leading question, "Why me? You must have loads of people working for you?"

"Not as many as you might think, and it got really complicated over the last few months."

She turns to her laptop. Syd, who is still sitting on the edge of her bed, disappears and is replaced with a picture of a front page of the Guardian from January. The headline story is about plain clothes officers infiltrating various groups; protesters, activists and political parties. They were accused of starting families, taking lovers and living second lives while watching various people of interest. Not legal, but sanctioned by the law. I had been aware of the story, but not given it a lot of my attention.

"Undercover work has been suspended," Alice states simply, "now we have no one to keep eyes and ears on vulnerable people, people who may be in a similar position to the one you and your friends were in."

I think I can see were this going, and I don't like it. The screen changes at a press of a key from Alice and a second news article appears, a headline and a photo of a group of environmentalists - all dreadlocks and swathes of ethnic clothes. An area of the photo has been highlighted, picking out a picture of a single person with his arm around a woman wearing a Levellers tee shirt and an oversized hat. The picture is grainy and it is not a full view of his face, someone has circled his partial profile with blue pen. The same blue pen has written a name in the margin - but it's bloody not, it's Trevor, or Simon - whatever the name says. I knew him from 1986, he followed me from town to town, keeping track of my movements, trying to befriend me, worming his way into my group of friends. He even went so far as to start a relationship with Shelley, Grace's best friend from college, just to get closer to me. Seeing him again leaves a bad feeling in the pit of my stomach, along with the other unsettling events of the last day. I really need a cigarette. "So, you want me to go undercover?"

"Not exactly. We want you to be our eyes and ears."

"How's that different?"

"Because everyone will know about it, it will all be above board. That's why we wanted someone who already knows the family, and who knows a bit about us. You are the only person who fits that particular skillset, you can give everyone the benefit of your experience."

I'm still not really following, I can't properly remember the last time I saw Syd or Grace before today. Actually, that's not true, I could tell you the exact date, but I'm not in regular contact now and I live miles away from them. I don't see how I am in a position to be of any practical use, unless Syd was being moved closer to where I live. "So, she'll be coming to live near me?"

"Not exactly, she'll have the same arrangement as you – going back to live at home."

"Well how will I…?"

The penny gradually begins to drop, she couldn't really mean that though, could she? I open my mouth to speak, then close it again as my thought processes try to catch up with the information I have been given.

"I'll let you figure it out, I need to go and talk to Sydney before she worries herself to death. Help yourself to tea and coffee and ask Mrs Baker if you need anything else."

"But…"

I don't really know what 'but' is; I let it hang there as I watch Alice leave the room. I sit where I am as the last conversation filters into my brain. I think I understand what Alice is suggesting, but how would that work? And what awful thing is Syd supposed to have done? I pour another mug of tea and take it outside where my gaze is drawn once again to the shadows of the clouds as they morph across the landscape. I finger the packet of cigarettes in my pocket and take a deep breath.

Syd

The door clicks open and the woman who had met her when she arrived came into the room. She was smiling and trying to look reassuring, but it was not enough to quell Sydney's rising sense of panic.

"Where am I? Who are you? Why am I here?" there are no pauses for answers because she doesn't really expect any.

"Hi Sydney, I'm Alice. I'm sorry, I can't answer all your questions right now, but I can tell you that you won't be here any longer than you need to be. We'll come to the why in a moment, first though, do you have everything you need for now? Do you want a change of clothes or anything to eat and drink?"

"No, I'm fine."

Actually, some clean underwear would be good, but she wasn't about to start asking for things. Her leggings and baggy black sweatshirt would last another day or two. Also, she was hungry, but didn't want to be indebted to these people, whoever they are.

"That's good, but do let us know if you need anything, we want you to be comfortable."

"Are you MI5? Can I call my mum? Do I get a lawyer?"

"You'll be able to speak to your mum soon, I promise. And no, we're much lower profile than MI5, I don't think a lawyer would be of much use to you at the moment, we have special jurisdiction in certain cases. Besides, we're just trying to help sort out a problem – and you have a big problem, Sydney."

She comes further into the room, pulls the chair away from the desk and sits down.

"What problem? Apart from being kidnapped and held hostage?"

"I'm sorry, it's how we operate and I know it's not always pleasant. Your laptop is the problem."

"How is my laptop a problem?" Sydney tried to think what she might have done, either deliberately or accidentally, that could cause a problem this big. Nothing came to mind. College work, browsing, exchanges on social media – God, was that it, was it because of groups she followed or posts she liked on Facebook? Greenpeace, Occupy and a couple of others. Surely they couldn't arrest everybody that had looked at those pages, could they?

"Is it the Occupy stuff? I didn't do anything illegal you know."

"No, it's nothing to do with that. Your laptop was used, 3 days ago, to hack into CIA's mainframe and download sensitive data. I hardly need to say that they are very upset, although they haven't traced the hack back to its source yet. We did and it led us to you, we've thrown down some false leads for them to follow. Don't ask me how, the tech guys started to explain it but it was too confusing for me. Suffice to say they put down a trail of digital breadcrumbs that should buy us a little time, so we can try and get this sorted out before they find their way back to you. Whoever did it went to a lot of trouble to cover their tracks. I don't want to make too many assumptions, but I haven't found any evidence yet to indicate your hacking skills are at that level."

"I wouldn't even know where to start, are you certain it was my computer?"

"Yes, who else has access to it?"

"Other people in the house borrow it from time to time, and Rick used it to…." She tailed off. Rick had used her laptop on Tuesday night, he said he had an assignment to finish, she had gone to bed and left him to it.

She had met Rick at the start of term. She had bunked off an English lecture for a student union meeting, to show solidarity with the Occupy protesters. Rick had been there, long hair and frayed jeans with a baseball cap pulled down to his eyebrows. He had caught her eye and she was pleased when he approached her afterwards and asked if she wanted to go for a drink, not the student union bar but a quiet old-fashioned pub in town. After several drinks she found him charming, funny, interesting, and committed to the same causes as her. One thing led to another and they ended up leaving the pub and going back to her flat, where he spent the night. They had spent most nights there subsequently, but it now struck her that she doesn't know that much about him.

She doesn't know what course he was doing beyond the vaguest of descriptions, or what year of his studies he is in. She realised now that she doesn't even know his surname. All she knew was that he was good-looking and had paid her more attention than she thought was possible, and she had been sharing her bed with him for the last couple of weeks. She guessed she could add bastard to his list of attributes now though, to help redress the balance of the known and unknown.

"Rick used the laptop."

"Tell me about Rick."

She told Alice everything she knew, which didn't amount to much. She assumed that Alice didn't want to know how satisfactory a lover he was, or how good he looked after a shower. Alice listened carefully and interjected at various points with seemingly random questions:

"Can you tell me which things he might have touched or handled in your room?"

"Where does he live?"

"Have you got any pictures of him on your phone?"

"What accent does he have?"

"What places did you go together?"

Sydney quickly realised that her answers to all of these questions were totally inadequate, she began to feel embarrassed that she had let someone she knew so little about into her life so trustingly. Alice tried to reassure her,

"It's okay, you're doing really well. We've got enough to start a good profile on Rick now, hopefully you've given us enough to keep the Americans off your back."

There were more questions, some with answers, most without.

Finally Alice asked, "How are you feeling? Do you want to grab something to eat now? There's some rather good veggie lasagna on the go today."

Syd finally admitted to herself that she was ravenous,

"Yes please, that would be good."

"Okay, I'll get someone to bring it to you. I'm sorry but I have to leave you again, I'll be back as soon as I can, it won't be too long okay?"

"Okay."

Syd found the woman's tone and demeanour reassuring, although she was feeling defiled and deflated. It was clear from the questions she had asked that she thought Rick might not be who he had claimed to be, but someone who had taken advantage of her naivety and gullibility. She felt stupid.

"Fuck!" she muttered under her breath as the door closed. She really wanted to talk to Mum now, the woman had promised she would be able to. She would ask again when she saw her. She wasn't sure what Mum was going to think of this – any of it. She hoped she wouldn't be too mad, last time they spoke it had been cursory and brief as she had other things to do, probably waiting for Rick to come round. That had been over a week ago now, although they hadn't had any prolonged contact for a while before that either. Syd wasn't really an 'I want my mum' sort of a girl, but right now she found that she really missed her and needed her; she wished she was here.

CHAPTER 5
Arrival

"So, this is how it is," starts Alice, "you'll be in a hotel near to Grace's home. Sydney will be going back to live with her – you know that drill. Your school knows you are not going to be in for a while, so no need for you to contact them, in fact it would probably be best to keep a low profile for the moment in terms of contacting anybody. Your job will be to keep an eye on things until it all settles down, checking in regularly, making sure everyone is okay."

I am not surprised at the efficiency with which my work has been reorganized, I am more surprised that Alice still thinks I am the right person for this job.

"You'd trust me with that?"

"I'd trust you with my life, you're honest and good. Plus, I've still got leverage."

"You bastard," I half smile as I finish the last mouthful of my lasagna, "even after all this time?"

"Yes, even after all this time."

"But I can't spy on Grace, it would seem wrong."

"Nobody said anything about spying."

"You said I'd be watching them."

"Yes, but they will know you are, it will be with their knowledge and consent. We've been trying to do things differently recently, a bit less of the cloak and dagger stuff."

"Won't they mind? I haven't been in touch for ages."

"They won't mind, not once they know what the alternatives are."

"What are the alternatives?"

"The Americans find out that it was Sydney's laptop that was used, which they will do eventually, they find her and deal with it themselves."

"That would be bad would it?"

"They really wouldn't want it, let's leave it at that."

I believe her, although I tell Alice that I am still unsure about the whole 'watching Grace and Syd' scenario. What if they don't want me hanging about? What if Grace's husband doesn't want me around? Ed's a nice enough guy, but even so… and anyway, what would I even be watching for?

Alice assures me that Ed, won't be bothered. I don't know how she could possibly be that confident about it, but she is. She tells me that she is sure Grace would prefer 'the devil she knows.' I am not sure if that is a complimentary turn of phrase, but I'll let it go. As for the what, it is anything unusual or worth noting. This seems unbelievably vague to me, but I go with it. Mostly, she tells me, I will be offering moral support as someone they know who has been there, seen it, done it and got the tee shirt. This makes more sense, even if I don't think our situations are over similar.

I feel as if my life may be coming unstuck, trapped in a series of events I have no control over. Other people's lives overlap with mine, crisscrossing through my own plans and taking me off course. I don't know if the tingle of excitement I am feeling under my nervousness is what I needed, to shake me out of my rut, or if I have been cleverly manipulated into my current position and no good will come of it.

"I need to sort some things out now, I'll see you very soon. You'll get a chance to ask Sydney yourself, if she says 'no' we'll think again, ok?" She smiles reassuringly as she leaves the room.

I am left sitting by myself in the sterile room, watched by unhidden cameras from every angle. Like a shit Big Brother, but with no cash prize if I'm lucky enough to come through it unscathed. I walk back to my room thinking I may read or have a lay down, but I know I won't settle to either. I grab a sweatshirt and my MP3 player and find my way back to the main entrance where I sit on the path at the side of the building and listen to an 80's playlist which seems to mostly comprise of Bauhaus and Killing Joke. Still staples after all the years that have passed, and still good. I finally succumb to the temptation in my pocket.

It tastes foul, the first two inhalations make me cough and I feel dizzy. Then the familiarity of the action kicks in, it feels good in my hand and I start to enjoy it. 'Just the one' I tell myself, although as long as I am here, I know this will be an over-ambitious promise. In the depths of my brain neurons are firing up and remembering how much I enjoy this, how good it feels. I watch the plumes of exhaled smoke rolling upwards and disguising themselves against the background of clouds.

The warmth of the afternoon is fading quickly now, shadows lying long in the sparse vegetation and creating large pools of shade. A movement in the distance catches my eye, a glint of light from a car travelling along the final run-in to the gate. It is the only thing that has happened since I came outside and I stand up for a better view, watching as it crawls towards me, taking my earphones out and observing. It glides silently at first, then the gradually increasing sound of its engine and the crunch of wheels on tarmac announce the cars imminent arrival.

It is the same blue car I arrived in yesterday, growing bigger and moving faster at an exponential rate. It reaches the gate and the guard lets it in. It has parked on the gravel before the gate has finished closing. Carl steps out of the driver's side. The passenger door opens as, simultaneously, I hear the swooshing sound of the doors behind me. I glance around to see Alice walking towards the car, I turn back and there, standing by the open car door, is Grace. She has one hand resting on the car roof, one foot still in the car, her eyes are wide and there is a sense of panic about her. Also, with a look that could kill, she is staring directly at me, "What the fuck are you doing here? What the fuck is going on? Where's Syd?"

Alice

'Well, that could have gone better,' she thought. She supposed it also could have gone worse, after all the best laid plans and all that.

They are sitting in the meeting room in uncomfortable silence while drinks are procured and a live feed from Syd's room has her joining them, virtually for now, largely for Grace's reassurance. She is anxious to speak to her and Alice has had to use her not insignificant negotiating techniques to persuade her to wait until they have had a chance to talk first. She thinks she might still need yet more of her skills to move things forward.

Grace sits looking at the monitor, Syd is sitting on the edge of the bed in her tee shirt drinking a cup of tea. She looks calm as she carefully sips it. Grace subconsciously takes a sip of her own tea each time Syd does. She asks;,"Why's she here? Is this something to do with him?" She points with a nod of her head, not even attempting to make eye contact.

Alice would have rather she had seen Grace alone first, but what had happened in the car park had happened, it was just one of those things.

"No, he's here because I asked him to be. He's doing me a favour – I'll explain later."

Now Alice gives a thorough overview of why Sydney is here, emphasizing the seriousness of the situation. She tells her how they are trying to resolve the issue. She is not sure whether to talk about the CIA interest, but decides it's best if everybody knows everything. Grace listens carefully without interrupting, right up to the point that Alice tells her about the arrangements for Syd to return home.

"What about her degree?"

"She'll pick it up at your local university, it's all been arranged. You and Syd will be offered the support of someone who has been through a similar experience. It's someone you already know, which will help, I think it's for the best until things have been resolved."

Grace is still clearly unhappy, which is understandable in the circumstances. A dawning realisation has occurred to her.

"So he's the person supporting us?" She makes eye contact this time, but there is nothing friendly about it.

"If you would like that, yes."

"Is this what happened to him?"

"More or less, yes."

"What did he do?"

"We can't really talk about that right now, later maybe. Now I think it's time to get Sydney in, she needs to see you and I'm sure you want to see her. I'll explain everything once you've seen that she's okay, she's scared and you're worried so let's not keep her waiting."

"She won't like it – I don't like it."

"We can talk about it. We'll do our best to make it work, but I hope you understand how serious this is."

Grace grudgingly acknowledges the gravity of the situation, then waits as Alice goes to collect Syd. She sees Grace staring silent daggers across the room as she leaves and hopes again that this is going to work. She knows that she will be watched on the monitor as she collects Sydney and brings her to the meeting room and puts on her most confident air of authority.

Syd enters the frigid silence of the room and hurries to her mum, even before the door has shut she wraps her arms around her then stands back and grips her hands. The relief on both their faces is palpable and they immediately start to talk over one another.

"I'm sorry mum, I didn't mean for this to happen."

"Are you okay, has anyone hurt you?"

They rapidly establish an order for their exchange.

"Mum, I'm sorry – I didn't do anything, I was stupid."

"Syd, as long as you're okay, that's all that matters."

They are still standing, neither wanting to move away from the other.

"What's going to happen, have they told you? I've been locked up since I got here. Can I come home now?"

"Locked up? What, in a cell?"

"Kind of, well no, it's more like that awful hall of residence room I was in last year - but with no door handle or windows."

"But you're okay?"

"I'm fine, I'm sorry mum, I know you've got lots on, I didn't mean for this to happen."

"Enough with the apologising. You're coming home, it's not your fault, none of it is."

"It is though. I was stupid."

"No, you were used."

Grace gives Syd a hug and a tear runs down her face.

"Mum, I'm scared, I don't really know what's happening."

"It's going to be okay, we'll sort it out."

Now she addresses the room in her best, seasoned, take-no-prisoners, teachers voice, "We need to talk now, give us some privacy."

There is no reason for them not to have the time to themselves, they need it. She knows Bob will tell her if the conversation is anything that she needs to be aware of.

CHAPTER 6
Talk

Syd is sitting with Grace – who has been glaring at me the whole time, as if this is all my fault, as though I am personally responsible for everything. To be honest I'm glad when she suggests we give them a minute. I want to tell her that I'm not 'one of them', I'm not in the gang. I don't think she'd believe me right now. Also, it's not strictly true, I am now. I have, unknowingly, been at their mercy all of my adult life, it just didn't really hit home until yesterday.

I make straight for the outside and light a cigarette as soon as I am through the door. It is better than the last one. I suck greedily on it, my hand trembling slightly, then turn to Alice who has followed me outside. "This won't work, she hates me."

"She doesn't, she's just shocked and a little scared."

"Didn't you see the way she looked at me? I don't even know what it is you want me to do really, what I am supposed to do, or how long for."

"It's just what we said earlier, we'll talk about it again later, together. It shouldn't be for long, just until the storm passes, you know how it goes?" She gently puts her hand on my arm and smiles, "It'll be fine, they just need a friendly face."

I am not convinced, but I wish I could at least have a chance to talk to Grace, to explain that it isn't my idea, that I never even really had a choice. Alice leaves my side and I hear the doors close behind me,

I light another cigarette and breathe in some more smoke as I gaze absently at the sky. A hand on my arm surprises me, I look around and realise that Grace must have come out as Alice went in.

"I thought you'd given up."

I look reflexively at the cigarette still in my hand then back at Grace.

"I have, but needs must. How are you? Or is that a stupid question?"

"Stupid question."

"How's Syd?"

"She's still cross, I can't blame her. Why are you here? Where even are we?"

I try to explain, as simply as possible, how I was coerced into coming back, how Alice persuaded me to return. I tell her I didn't know anything about it being to do with her or Syd until I got here, and try to convince her that this was definitely not my idea. She still looks distrustful;,she wraps her arms around herself and shivers. Her hair is shorter now, with unashamed streaks of grey, while her face is still the same mixture of beautiful imperfections and hidden humour – very well hidden today. She is still as quirky and beautiful as when I first met her, standing beside me in a baggy brown jumper and faded jeans. I feel an urge to put my arms around her, hold her tight and tell her everything will be all right. Even though she is still not making eye contact with me, I am on the verge of convincing myself that I could and should do this when Alice returns,

"Shall we talk?"

Grace turns and follows wordlessly as I put out the stub of my cigarette then tag along ten feet behind them.

Back inside Grace sits alongside Syd, facing Alice across the table. I place myself to one side, feeling extraneous. Alice lays bare what has happened, what needs to happen next and what that will be like. I listen without interruption as she explains that I will be around to support them and to act as a conduit to her if anything is needed. Nobody asks anything, letting Alice explain it all. Syd's face changes by degrees – she is clearly biting her tongue. When Alice comes to an end and asks if there are any questions she speaks out, "But I didn't bloody do anything."

"I believe you," answers Alice, "that's why I don't want you to stay here, this place is only ever a last resort. However, it wasn't our national security database that was compromised. I'm doing everything I can to keep this under wraps while we sort it out, and you've been really helpful in that. If we're lucky we can stay a couple of steps ahead of everyone else until it's over."

"But it wasn't me, can't you just tell them that?"

"I can, and I will when it's the right time. But I can only do so much to protect you."

"Protecting?" I blurt out, "What? So I'm like a body guard?"

"No, just an observer, I'll provide bodyguards when they're necessary."

Now it's Grace's turn to look alarmed, "Might they be?"

"Probably not, we're getting a bit ahead of ourselves. I just need to make sure we all know what needs to happen for now."

I share Grace's concern, nobody mentioned bodyguards before, and even though it was me that bought it up, I can't get the thought out of my mind. Alice explains the rules to Grace and Syd and how things will be managed. I am already familiar with the routine and zone out, finally excusing myself to take a toilet break. Old habits are returning with a vengeance and I use the opportunity to go outside for a smoke before returning to the room. Fuck it, I'll stop again once I'm away from here.

I have only just lit up when Grace comes out, she walks over and stands beside me.

"Hi, where's Syd?"

"Talking to that woman – Alice?"

"Yeah, Alice. Syd's pissed off isn't she?"

"So am I, have you been working here all the time I've known you?"

"God no, I don't work here at all. I had to come here the same as Syd, just before you first met me. That's why Julia...Alice, thinks I might be able to help now."

"Might you?"

"I don't know, but I will if I can. I want to."

Grace appears to believe what I have told her, her anger and mistrust seem to be abating - slightly,

"If I get hold of that boyfriend I'll skin him."

I have the gist of this part of the story now, and I don't blame Grace for feeling that way.

"I'll hold him down for you."

"Thanks." She pauses then tentatively asks, "So, is this the same as what happened to you?"

"Kind of, I came here, but I think I bought it a bit more on myself."

"It's no wonder you were so depressed when I first met you."

She is definitely mellowing a bit from earlier, and it's good to be talking again. She's right, I was at a low point when we first met all those years before. It was hard. I had lost all my friends, one of them was dead. I was in serious shit and I had to go and live back with my parents. What was not to be depressed about? Looking back, I know it needed to happen, it was for the best. But I still feel a mixture of anger, sadness, guilt and grief whenever I think about it. I have been thinking about it a lot over the last 24 hours or so. I change the subject.

"Won't Ed mind me hanging about?"

"Only if you're going to be hanging about in Leicester."

"Eh?"

"With him and his new partner."

"Oh God, Grace, no he didn't? I didn't know. I thought you two were right for each other."

I know this is what you're supposed to say, but actually I had never really warmed to Ed. For a start how can you really trust someone whose proper name is Edward. Secondly, I had visited Grace shortly before Syd was born, when we were still in more regular contact, and I'd seen a side of him I didn't like.

At the time I had been dating a beautician called Phoebe– and yes, I do know that I was punching above my weight, but I am nothing if not ambitious. She hadn't thought my suggestion of visiting my ex was odd, so we had made a weekend of it.

Ed had been his usual self, knowing everything about everything, which I have to admit I found annoying. But I didn't want to risk alienating Grace by badmouthing him, so I had always kept my opinion to myself. From the start he had been over attentive to Phoebe, taking every opportunity to talk to her, standing close, putting his hand on her elbow, leaning in to talk to her. His eyes did not wander, they stayed firmly attached to Phoebe.

Of course, Phoebe was oblivious – or so she claimed later. But I watched as he virtually ignored Grace the whole weekend, saying things like 'I'm sure you two have loads to catch up on' as he led Phoebe into the garden on some pretext or another. Grace had a full, round stomach and was clearly finding life uncomfortable at times. I thought she looked wonderful, but Ed barely looked at her the entire time we were there.

In the evening, after a pleasant meal and a few glasses of wine, we were sitting around the table waiting for the food to settle before attacking the clearing up. Ed had excelled himself by stopping the conversation so he could put on an album by The Eagles, then went on to explain to Phoebe, at great length, why Glenn Frey was one of the greatest guitarists alive – if not the best ever.

I mean seriously? The Eagles? I'll admit Boys of Summer is a classic; but that's Don Henley, not Glenn Frey. He didn't stop explaining even when I starting helping Grace with the dishes. The weekend wasn't a washout, but it left me feeling uncomfortable, the way he tried to flirt with Phoebe – and The Eagles! I never talked about any of this with Grace, what would I have said that wouldn't have upset her? I split up with Phoebe a couple of months later when she dumped me for a firefighter.

Grace snorts, "I thought me and you were too, once upon a time. Anyway, I'm glad he's gone, I've got my life to myself again, no more hanging about while he pops off and does a triathlon, or wondering when he'll get back from the golf course. If that's even where he ever was."

"What a dick, that sounds awful. "

"It was, it still is if I'm honest. It will actually be good to have Syd home for a bit."

"Yes, and me too apparently, I hope that's not going to cramp your free-living style. I won't make you listen to The Eagles."

Grace looks momentarily confused, then manages a smile,

"No, I'm already planning how to explain this to our nosey neighbour. You'll really pique her interest when you keep turning up."

I laugh and am about to say something witty in reply when Alice appears.

"Sorry to interrupt, I need to have a word with Grace."

She then informs me that I should 'just pop and see Carl for a minute', who's waiting for me inside'.

I have no idea why Carl might need to see me, but I go in anyway, where Carl is indeed waiting for me. He leads me to one of the smaller offices, it is sparsely decorated with a single table and two chairs, one of which he sits on. I follow his lead and sit on the other, facing him.

He looks serious, intense. He makes eye contact with me and doesn't break it once during the whole time we are together, I'm not even sure if he blinked.

"Alice said you were worried that you might need to offer protection."

"Ah, well not exactly."

"Whatever, listen carefully to what I'm about to tell you. I'm going to keep it as simple as I can."

"Okay."

"Good. First, you are to contact Alice if you see anything at all that you think is unusual or suspicious. If you're not sure, contact Alice. If you are worried, contact Alice. I will be nearby, I will decide if anything is worth worrying about or not, your job is to .."

"Tell Alice?"

"Good, you're getting it." There is no trace of humour in this.

"Second, if you are in a conflict situation you need to get out of it, run, hide, anything – but do everything and anything you can to get away. The people who are likely to be involved will have combat training, you are not a fighter so don't try. Go to a busy area if you can and make as much noise as possible, people who are going to do bad things don't usually like an audience"

"Bad things?"

"Do I really need to elaborate, use your imagination."

I try to, honestly though, it doesn't make me feel any better.

"Lastly, in the event that you have absolutely no choice, go for the soft spots, eyes, testicles, nostrils, ears. Anything to district them long enough to give you a chance to get away or call Alice. Preferably both."

I didn't feel nervous before, but I do now.

"Okay, got it."

"You'll be fine, I'll never be far away, and Alice has a great number of resources at her disposal if she needs them, that's why you need to call her if anything is going on. If we are in a difficult situation I will do everything I can to keep everybody safe, including you. In that event, make sure you follow my lead and follow my orders."

"Okay, do as I'm told, run away shouting and call Alice, got it."

The levity of my answer belies the undercurrent of nervousness I am now feeling at the thought of having to fight off bad guys. Carl however appears nonchalant and unconcerned.

Carl stands up and puts his hand on my shoulder, squeezing gently with a firm grip.

"All good then. I'm sure none of this pep talk will be necessary, we don't usually get any interference from other agencies, but Alice likes to cover her bases, consider yourself trained."

He walks to the door and steps out to where Alice, Syd and Grace are passing. He joins them walking towards the main entrance and I follow on a few steps behind. Sydney has a bag and a scowl that would scare the devil.

"All ready," smiles Alice, "Carl will take you home and I'll be in touch soon." She looks at me, "We've got a couple of things to sort out before you get going, if that's okay?"

I say goodbye to Grace and Syd telling them I'll see them again later. Syd does not look thrilled at the prospect, Grace manages a smile and a 'see you later'. Then Carl walks towards the door jangling the car keys as he marches towards the car. I am led back inside for a briefing which is so thorough and detailed that I am left reeling. How long ago did they start planning this? I wonder if it's an old plan that has been adapted, but so much of it is specific to Grace, Syd and me that I know it must have been put together this weekend.

Mostly the plan just seems to be me hanging about in a hotel for a week or two, visiting Grace and Syd each day and reporting back to Alice at set times on how everything is going. I am to let her know if we need anything or if anything unexpected happens. I am not to contact school, or parents or friends. I am asked to make a list of things I would like collected from my flat and given a credit card with my name on, to use as I please. I am then dispatched to collect my bag and meet Alice outside.

I go to the front of the building and light another cigarette as I walk towards Alice.

"You must call me if anything happens, anything no matter how insignificant. My number has been added to your phone contacts - under Alice - you can call it any time of the day or night, someone will always answer."

I am about to ask how they added the number to my phone while it was in my pocket the whole time, then remember it was never actually my phone and stop myself.

"Why's it such a big deal anyway? Surely the hack has been stopped or blocked or whatever it is they do by now?"

"Because nobody knows what, if anything, was downloaded."

"I see, secret flash drives and the CIA, it is all a bit cloak and dagger really though, isn't it?"

"Let's just say it's sensitive and leave it at that shall we? Here's your ride, I'll be in touch soon."

I mull this over as a car pulls up and the door is opened. I am driven away across the empty moors by a Carl-alike, smiling politely but about as talkative as the original, to my new temporary home. I look over my shoulder as we leave, Alice has gone back inside and the clouds have built up into a tower of billowing balloons on the horizon. I am glad to be leaving.

I look at the car radio, then decide I'm really not in the mood for chatty DJ's playing songs by Sad Girls and Boys Who Cry (as Spongebob Squarepants would describe the bands that are currently dominating the airwaves). I plug myself into my MP3 player and set it to play a random selection of Bruce Springsteen songs; these are familiar favourites, I close my eyes and settle down for the journey.

Alice

She rubs her temples with her fingertips before retrieving her glasses from the top of her head and looking back at the screen, where a steady stream of information and messages is being relayed to her.

She hopes that they have acted quickly enough, although she doesn't know how they could have done things any quicker, for now she is sure they have done enough to stay one step ahead. Sending Syd home was a gamble, but ultimately it was in her best interests. If only so much wasn't hanging on hopes and wishes. Everything nowadays happened so fast, it was easy to lose the advantage. She was as certain as she could be that they had the edge for now. Her certainty stemmed from the fact that she hadn't received any formal requests for sharing of information yet. But it was inevitable that they would come, and she would have to decide how to deal with them when they did. Another problem for another day.

She hadn't been doing this for as many years as she had without developing a healthy amount of scepticism and paranoia. In her experience there were only two reasons people didn't ask for information; either because they didn't know they needed it, or because they already had it.

Sighing, she looked at the clock then picked up her phone. Whichever way it was going to go there was nothing else she could do right now. Hopefully they would have some luck with the mysterious boyfriend, Rick. Perhaps they would get a break, at least a bit more luck than they had so far. In spite of the whole team working on face ID, prints and CCTV footage from in and around Sydney's flat, they were still drawing a blank. His fingerprints were not on their database and his face had been permanently shaded with a peaked cap or a hood.

She called Carl and briefed him on what she needed, smiling as he listened attentively then repeated back verbatim what she had said to him, without being prompted. She had already received a succinct but informative report from him,

'Safely in situ, all delivered. Will keep up obs.'

This was followed by his own throwaway comment'

'I am now going to gorge on takeaway food and sleep in the car for a week – pay rise?'

She deleted the second part of the message then leaned back in her chair and closed her eyes.

CHAPTER 7
Story

If I was a superstitious person I might have seen this coming, the signs were there in the echoing of major events of 1986 – aka 'the year my life turned upside down.'

In 1986 the explosion and subsequent meltdown at the Chernobyl power plant in Russia had dominated the news and people had panicked about the safety of nuclear power. Then, in March this year, Fukushima power plant in Japan was damaged by an earthquake. Not enough to be dangerous, but enough to render the plant susceptible to the tsunami that engulfed it in the wake of the tremors.

There was another world cup, with England once again failing to lift the trophy. In fact, not even managing to move on from the group stages this time.

While Prince Andrew and Sarah Ferguson had provided the royal wedding in the 80's, this time around it was Prince William and Catherine Middleton who tied the knot in a taxpayer funded jamboree in April.

The unrest of the riots in August would have seemed portentous too, only they were largely missed by me as I holidayed miserably alone in Greece.

So many echoes of that summer when Lisa, Sarah, Jo, Stewart and me found that cylinder on the train tracks. Unguarded and unsecured

- well, practically unsecured. We had taken it, in a misguided attempt to make sure it couldn't be used to cause any harm – somewhat ironically as it turned out. Of course people got hurt, we were tracked down, taken away and locked up, apart from Lisa. We should have just left it of course, I know that now. But life doesn't work like that, hindsight is exactly what it says it is.

Right now I don't know how I feel. My life has been safe for so long, tethered by routine, familiarity and inertia. Now it has changed again, it turns out that safety was just an illusion and I am standing in a hotel room on the outskirts of a strange town, surrounded by strangers.

In truth my life had, until now, been humdrum and undemanding. I had thought I liked it that way, but these recent events had added an element of spontaneity and mystery that I probably needed, to give me an incentive to make changes in my life. Maybe this would be a catalyst. Maybe it would shake me out of my comfort zone and into a place where I would be able to move on to a new chapter in my life, one where I wasn't always looking timidly over my shoulder and going with the flow.

In front of me is a meagre selection of neatly packed boxes containing the bits of my life that I had asked Alice for. They had been transported while I travelled, to be reunited with me here at the hotel. I wondered idly how they had got into my flat, they hadn't asked for the key. I dismiss the thought as soon as It comes into my head;,of course they can get into my flat, why would I think otherwise? I could see at a glance that whoever had been charged with this task had also used their initiative and included things that I had omitted to ask for, like a coat and some spare boots. Otherwise the selection of books, my laptop, and other personal items are functional. What's missing are the bits and pieces, the personal objects that make a home; the shells on the ledge, the painting of the beach I got from a local artist, the pieces of me. This is temporary, things will go back to normal, I'm trying hard to think of it as an adventure.

I think of Grace and wonder if I should visit, my car has also been conveniently relocated for me and is waiting in the car park. I check the time and decide that Grace and Syd probably have plenty of things to talk about without me hanging around. I look at the menu for the hotel restaurant and decide none of it is what I want, even if it can go on expenses. I go out in search of a chip shop.

Before long I am sitting in my car watching Saturday night start to flock past in its finest glad rags. Drunken boys and laughing girls in pairs and groups, all heading towards the town centre. A parade of youthful hedonism, preloaded and ready for what the night might bring. Watching them makes me feel older than I am. My phone rings and I wipe my greasy fingers on my jeans then swipe the screen, still managing to leave a smudge across the glass. It's Grace, "Hi, are you busy?"

"No, not at all," I look at the smear then glance up at a group of scantily clad young women walking raucously past, "not busy at all. Are you okay?"

"No."

"Of course not, stupid question, sorry." I don't know what to say next. Grace saves me.

"Can we talk? Can you come over? I really need someone to talk to right now."

"Sure, no problem. I'll need to figure out how to get to you, it's been a while."

"Where are you?"

I tell her and she gives me a brief set of instructions, it turns out I am already in the right direction and I find my way after a couple of turns, eventually recognising the route from my previous visit several years ago. It is an anonymous semi-detached house in a tidy close of 70s built houses with open, manicured front gardens.

As I approach the front door, I can hear my own footsteps exploding on the path and my hands feel too big, nothing feels right. It intensifies when Grace opens the door just as I lift my hand to ring the bell, her eyes are red and she has worry written into every line and crease on her face. She is still wearing the same clothes as earlier, jeans and a jumper, but has added a pair of pink fluffy slippers. Wordlessly she steps aside and lets me in.

Grace's house has all the things that are missing from my hotel room; clutter on the hall table, photos on the wall, sticky notes by the front door with reminders of things to take and tasks that need doing. I follow her into the kitchen where takeaway menus and recipes are stuck to the fridge with an eclectic selection of magnets, including one from my very own seaside home town which I remember sending many years ago. There is a brightly coloured jigsaw taking up the dining table, a mess of pieces spread around the completed edges. There are small fragments of the picture assembled, just waiting for the other 400 or so pieces to join them.

"Have you eaten?"

"Yeah, well kind of, I had some chips."

"Are you still hungry?"

"You still know me so well."

Grace manages a smile and pulls out some pasta and sauce, she boils the kettle and starts everything off. I stand and watch her as she cuts and fries the onion and peppers. Once it is all underway, she joins me leaning against the counter opposite me.

"I'm sorry if I was rude to you yesterday, I was in a bit of a state."

"No apology necessary. It must have been a real shock seeing Syd in that place. It's pretty grim."

"Tell me honestly, I need to know, are you one of those agents - or spies or whatever the hell they are?"

I can see that she is still unsure about how I fit into all this, I tell her, "No, I'm a just a teacher. I haven't seen that woman – Julia or Alice or whatever - since the 80s, I thought they'd forgotten about me. I kind of wish they had."

"So I can trust you?"

"I wouldn't blame you if you didn't, but yes. I have nothing to gain from this, she asked me to do it as a favour."

This is not quite true, I do have something to gain, maybe redemption, maybe closure. Mostly the chance to be free of the whole thing at last. I say none of this, and Grace appears to accept my answer as it is and visibly relaxes.

"How's Syd?"

"Shut in her bedroom."

"Poor thing, it must have been awful for her."

"Well, you would know apparently."

"It was a long time ago, and not the same situation. But yes, it was shit."

Grace stirs the sauce and starts to drain the pasta in a cloud of steam, she then spoons it into three bowls with a special spoon with serrated teeth, evidently for the specific purpose of dishing up pasta. I wonder to myself how these fragments of adulthood have passed me by, tiny things that hint at permanence and organisation. She pauses to wipe the condensation from her glasses then pours the sauce over the top and adds some cheese. The smell is sweet and subtle, taking over the kitchen and letting me know I am in a home, with Grace as its beating heart. In spite of the chips I had earlier I find I still have an appetite.

"Smells delicious."

"Good, we're going to eat this, then you're going to tell us everything."

"I don't know if…"

"Bullshit, we're all in this together now. All those things you couldn't or wouldn't tell me before, Syd needs to know them now if she's going to trust us -otherwise you'll just be 'one of them' to her. You owe me this."

I can feel myself slumping, I've spent years telling myself I couldn't talk about it 'for security reasons'. I remember laying with Grace in her single bed at her mother's house. Her parents had gone to work and her brother had gone somewhere, who cares where. I had taken the opportunity to leave the sofa bed and join her in her childhood bedroom.

We were both naked and sweaty, her arm was resting on my scrawny adolescent chest, she pulled her long curly hair back from her face and looked into my eyes;

"Tell me what I can do to help."

"You're doing it, you've done more than enough."

"But I don't feel like I have, there's something in you that's - I don't know? – broken."

"Thanks."

"Be serious, I can't help you if I don't know why these people are watching you. I want to do more."

I knew that she did, I wanted to tell her so badly, I really needed to share the thing that was eating me away from the inside. I so nearly did, not just then, but at other times too. I was so often on the verge of blurting it out, telling her all my secrets and binding her to my guilt and shame.

But I didn't, the thought of making her complicit had outweighed the notion. I knew they were watching and listening and I just couldn't risk it. I have often wondered what the result would have been if I had told her what had happened to me that summer. But I didn't, I bit my lip and closed my eyes until I felt Grace's arms wrap around me and thought that somehow, sometime, things might be better.

I realise now, with a sinking feeling, that this mystery has been eating at Grace for as long as I have known her. And now she needs to know, she deserves answers. I feel an extra layer of guilt settle over me, knowing that I have been oblivious to the confusion and hurt I have caused. If I had trusted her I could have stopped it at any time, but I chose not to.

There is nothing I could say now that would change the course of what happened in the last 25 years. My self-imposed exile is coming to an end, the world has moved on. I have never talked about what I did, my stupidity, my shame for my own recklessness, and the consequences, actual and potential. I surrender, "Okay."

"Good, beer?"

"Yeah, I think I'm going to need it."

Syd comes down to join us for the meal, she doesn't offer much in the way of conversation or make eye contact with me. Grace doesn't add much to the ambience either, after all, what is there to talk about apart from the obvious? For my own part I am mostly thinking about a discussion which hasn't happened yet.

Grace collects the empty plates and puts them on the side in the kitchen, and I start scanning the puzzle pieces we have eaten around, looking for a red striped piece. Syd gets up to excuse herself.

"No, stay Syd, we're about to hear a story. I think we both need to hear it."

Grace looks directly at me,

"And I think you need to tell it at last."

Syd rolls her eyes and reseats herself, then they both look at me expectantly. I finish my beer, dragging out the moment, not for dramatic effect, but to brace myself, then I begin,

"It was the end of summer and me and some friends went back to college to decorate the common room…."

Once I start it tumbles out of me, the whole chain of events, from finding the mysterious cylinder, to dragging it through the woods, to hiding it in the pond. Then to Lisa dying, about how Lisa was the best of us, someone who could have done anything. Over the years I have thought about her, all that promise and potential lost before she even had a proper chance to make her mark on the world.

I tell them about how the entire college was isolated, put into quarantine and the net closed around us until, eventually, I was taken to the centre – the same one we had just left - in the middle of the night. Leaving behind my life as I had known it up to that point. The wrenching uncertainty about what would happen, and the shock of what actually did happen. It is cathartic, finally telling untold secrets, things I couldn't and haven't ever told a living soul, things that I had lived in fear of for most of my adult life.

As I tell it the words fall out of my mouth. Syd and Grace don't interrupt and I relive the years of 1986 and 1987, articulating what has been locked inside my head since then. My story. I leave out some details, particularly the awful gruesomeness of Lisa's death, I thought it might be easier to remember after all these years, but the image of her laying, dying in a spreading pool of her own blood on the gravel path still haunts me. I feel a tear running down my cheek.

I stop telling my tale at the point I met Grace in my new college, living back at home with my parents, shellshocked and scared.

"You kind of know what happened after that."

"Syd doesn't."

So I continue, laying bare my fears and insecurity, about people being sent to spy on me and monitoring my movements, about being bugged and having my mail and phone calls monitored. I get to the part about leaving college and not being able or willing to move nearer to Grace. I feel vulnerable, finally exposing my stupidity and fears to the one person who I never wanted to see me like this. It feels as if it borders on paranoia at times, although it turned out I was right, they really had been tracking and watching me for all of those years. Which is how come I am here now. I finish, finally grinding to a halt.

"I'm sorry," I say, "so, so sorry." For a moment I think I might cry, I look down at the empty bottle I am holding in my lap.

"Do you need another beer?" asks Syd.

I nod and recompose myself while Syd gets one for me and one for herself from the fridge. Grace still has half a bottle, she puts it on the table and comes over to give me a hug, it feels good. It feels like the hug she gave me that morning all those years ago when I just needed someone to hold me and tell me it would be okay. Making things better even though they can't be right.

"I don't know what to say," Grace says, "I wish I'd known before. So many things make sense now."

"It's kind of hardcore," says Syd, "did you find the others?"

"No, I stopped looking. It felt easier to let sleeping dogs lie. I think I've spent over half my life scared that I might slip up, that I'll be found out."

"Is that what it's going to be like for me now?" Syd looks concerned.

"No, Alice thinks it'll all blow over," I tell her.

"Do you trust her?"

"She's always been straight with me, upfront."

Conversation turns to what we think is going to happen next. The short answer is that none of us know, we manage to drag our combined lack of knowledge or information out for an inordinate amount of time. Eventually, when the darkness outside starts to seep in through the windows, I realise that I am not going to be able to drive back to the hotel, having seen off several beers.

"Do you have a number for a taxi?" I ask.

"Oh god, I never even thought of that, says Grace, "I'm sorry. Why don't you stay over?"

"I don't want to be any bother, I'll get a cab."

"It's no bother, the sofa pulls out into a bed."

I accept graciously. Syd dismisses herself and goes back to her room while Grace collects pillows and a spare duvet. Together we unfold and make up the sofa bed, she looks at me from across the bed, "It really is good to see you, you're looking well," I tell her.

"You too. I wish I had known some of those things before, I know why you didn't tell me, but it would have helped me understand what you were going through at the time. Are you okay? You were upset earlier."

"Honestly, I don't know. It feels like a weight lifted, but I'm worried you'll think less of me, now that you know what I did."

"No, if anything I've got more respect, I can't believe you carried that on your own for all that time."

"I was ashamed, I killed Lisa."

"No, you didn't. Whoever left that thing on the tracks was to blame, not you."

"That's what Alice said, I still wish we'd left it where it was. Still, if wishes were horses…. Anyway, when did you and Ed split up?"

"Last year, when he announced he was moving out with his newer, younger model. A 27 year old secretary from his work."

"Are you okay?"

There's a sadness in her eyes that I want to fix, but know that I can't - it's not within my power to. But I see a steeliness too, the same look I had seen many times before. I knew that she would come through because Grace has always been determined and resilient.

"I'm doing better now, it was a huge shock, I never saw it coming. I never thought I would be the sort of person that needed antidepressants before."

"I wish you would have messaged me or called."

"I wasn't exactly proud that I'd been dumped for his younger mistress - or that he'd been seeing her for over a year without me knowing or suspecting a thing. The shit even asked me if I would tell Syd."

"Not good, what an idiot. You look great, and you've always been one of the nicest people I know, so his loss."

It's true, I look at Grace and see the beautiful woman my former girlfriend has become and I could kick myself for ever letting her go. I guess I am doomed to a life of idiocy.

"I don't and I'm not, I'm older, fatter and grumpier. Don't you try and smooth talk me."

For some reason this makes me laugh, it's the kind of thing Grace would have said when I first knew her at college, whenever I had had the temerity to compliment her. Grace laughs too, and for a moment the years drop away and the smile wipes away the cares, worries and woes that have sat on her face since yesterday.

"We'll talk again tomorrow," she says.

"Sure, it's been a long day," I yawn, "see you in the morning."

She goes upstairs and I pause by the bed, then quietly go to the front door and let myself out, leaving it slightly ajar. I take the cigarettes from my pocket and light one, watching the stars blink on and off as swiftly moving invisible whorls of clouds pass in front of them. There is a car parked across the street, in the shadows, it looks as if there could be someone in the driver's seat. Probably Carl, he said he would be nearby. I imagine Alice is on the case even now, trying to smooth things over and sort everything out. I don't know her well, but one thing I have discovered over the years is that she is meticulous, tenacious and good to her word.

When I go back in there is a pair of pyjamas on the bed, Ed's I presume, and the house is silent. My sleep is punctuated with vivid and confused images from the deep recesses of my memory, dragged back to the surface and denying me the peaceful night that should have been mine by rights, after unburdening myself at long last.

Syd

Creeping quietly down the stairs in her leggings and tee shirt to get a glass of water, she tries not to make a sound. Her bare feet on the carpet seem to make more noise than is possible in the stillness. She doesn't want to wake Mum's ex who is snoring in the back room, or mum either for that matter. She has done enough talking for now, it's time for some thinking. This is why she finds herself awake so early and unable to get back to sleep.

Her clothes and belongings are mostly in her student flat. They are probably still scattered carelessly about the place, like a landlocked Mary Celeste, after she had left so abruptly and unexpectedly. The woman, Alice, had told her they would be collected and delivered to her, except the laptop of course, that is in the process of being dismembered, dissected and probably destroyed. Her phone is back with her, apparently it is straightforward to clone every last image, message and call she has ever made. Now someone is busy trawling through everything that she had thought was private and personal, scouring them for hints and clues about who Rick really was, where he might be, maybe even why he had picked on her.

Not that her phone is much use anyway. She has been told, in no uncertain terms, that she is not to go onto social media or contact her friends for now. A tracking app has been added and they said they would be monitoring. She has no reason to disbelieve this, now her phone is merely a device for calling people and being called on – she may as well have one of those old-fashioned Nokias that everyone makes the memes about. She has gone over the events of the last few weeks in her mind, obsessively trying to work out how something like this could have happened to her. The answer she keeps coming to is that she is gullible and stupid. It hurts.

Looking back, she can see now the warning signs she missed in her infatuation with Rick, and could kick herself. All the things she should have noticed at the time;his reluctance to meet when she was with other people, only meeting off campus, the odd hours he kept;,the speed he answered her messages from his now disconnected number, as if he was waiting for them.

It still gives her a chill feeling when she thinks how easily she was whisked away to that strange prison in the middle of nowhere. It was seriously freaky, though maybe not as weird as that story mum's ex told them last night. It seemed like what had happened to him had pretty much messed up his entire life, and now the same is happening to her. She can't imagine never seeing her friends again and is determined not to let it have the same effect on her life as it clearly had on his.

She looks around the kitchen as she sips her glass of water, so familiar, and yet strangely off-kilter since dad buggered off. One less bunch of keys on the hooks, a single phone charging cable on the counter, no smoothie maker or coffee machine. Everything has been pared down to suit a single person – Mum. Maybe that was part of the problem, since Dad left Mum had been kind of distant and lethargic. She hadn't wanted to go away this summer and had stayed at home, reading and doing jigsaws mostly. It hadn't been a lot of fun and she had found it hard to connect with her at times. The truth was that she had been hurt by Dad leaving too, it had been the very time that they needed each other the most, but they had managed to drift silently apart instead. She can see that now, she can see it all too well.

As she gazes thoughtfully at the absence of things in the house, cogs start to grind in that part of her brain that keeps working whether you want it to or not, making subconscious connections that she cannot fathom or follow for now.

When they questioned her at the prison, she could remember only the bare minimum of details about Rick. Now she has time to really think small details are starting to come back. Nothing useful or helpful of course, just incidental details that she didn't realise she had taken in at the time.

He always wore the same make of boxer shorts and unbranded tee shirts. He would stand in the kitchen making coffee with the cafetière he had bought round after the first time he had stayed over

– he said it was a spare from his parents' house, but it looked brand new. That first time he stayed she had made him instant coffee and he left most of it to go cold. At the time she had thought he was being generous and kind when he bought the coffee maker, now it dawns on her that he had not done it for her but for himself, she was quite happy with coffee from the jar.

She sighed and tiptoed back upstairs as quietly as she could, it was still only 6.45, she had been awake on and off for much of the night and was hoping she would be able to get back to sleep for an hour or two before the day got properly underway.

CHAPTER 8
Walk

I am awake. I heard footsteps on the stairs earlier. I tried to tell from their sound if they were Grace's or Syd's. I think it was Syd, something intangible and intuitive, but I'm sure I'm right nevertheless. If it was Grace I would have gone into the kitchen and joined her, but I'm pretty sure Syd wouldn't want me standing in the kitchen in her dad's pyjamas making small talk early in the morning. I listen to her bare feet padding around in the kitchen, I really need to pee but will wait until the coast is clear. The need is getting more pressing and uncomfortable by the minute and it is a relief when I finally hear steps going back up the stairs. I go to the downstairs cloakroom and splash some water on myself at the sink and get dressed while I am in there. When I come out Grace is in the kitchen.

"Morning, tea and toast?"

"Yes please, have you got marmite?" I find myself staring at her bare feet which protrude from the frayed hem of her well-worn dressing gown. There is nothing sensual about this, nevertheless I find myself feeling aroused. I quickly busy myself by ineffectually helping in the kitchen, I would probably be more use if I knew where anything was.

"Did you sleep okay on the bed settee?"

"Fine thanks, you know me, I can sleep anywhere."

"You always could."

"It's a skill worth having, did you get much sleep?"

"It's definitely not a skill, and yes I slept fine – I was in my bed."

"That's not what I meant."

"I know, I woke up a couple of times in a panic. I could hear Syd moving around earlier, I don't think she slept so well. How did you do it for all those years?"

"I didn't. You remember what a bad way I was in when you first met me. It's gotten better over the years; I'd almost forgotten how bad it was until two days ago."

"Oh God, and now it's started again. Are you really okay?"

"I guess, I'm not completely sure what I'm meant to do now though. Are you going to work tomorrow?"

"I already rang in sick. You can stay here today, if you want."

"I need to go back to the hotel, all my clothes and stuff are there. I haven't even unpacked yet."

"Sounds like you, come back later and I'll make us some lunch."

"That sounds great, I'll take you up on it. I was worried I was going to be living off takeaways indefinitely."

"Isn't that what you usually do then?"

"No, I cook, just not very well and not every night. Plus my parents live up the road. You know how it is when you're on your own?"

As soon as the words leave my mouth I realise how insensitive this is, but Grace just smiles and nods.

"Sadly, yes."

"Sorry, I didn't mean…."

"It's okay, I'm getting used to it. Go on, clear off and let me get dressed in peace."

I drain my mug and put it by the sink with my plate.

"Okay, see you at lunchtime."

"Yes, see you. And thanks for last night."

"I didn't do anything."

"You did, I think maybe that Alice woman was right to ask you to do this, I think it's going to help Syd."

"She didn't exactly ask, I'm just glad I haven't made things worse. See you later."

I leave the house and walk out to the close. There is no sign of the car that had been parked there last night, a part of me thinks that I might have imagined it. Another part thinks probably not. I stand by my own car and take a cigarette from the packet. Half of them are gone now, I won't get any more after this – but it's a shame to waste them. I lean on the roof of the car and feel slightly light-headed after the first couple of puffs. It's a bright morning, dry with a smattering of clouds against the blue backdrop of the sky. The gardens in the close are still green, but there are definite hints of yellowing leaves and fading flowers that will presage the coming of autumn.

A white van is parked on a driveway diagonally opposite Grace's house. It has a good line of sight and there is no obvious building work going on right now. It could all be taking place inside of course, but just because I'm paranoid…. Further along the close is a house with a 'to let' sign, I think it would make an ideal spot to sit and watch the comings and goings in the close, but what do I know? I flick my cigarette end towards a drain, then retrace my route back to the hotel through the busy morning traffic.

The hotel reception area is bustling: leavers mingling with a freshly arrived coach full of people, a maze of luggage and a family with a small child in a buggy, waiting to pay their bill, all being crisscrossed by groups of all-you-can-eat breakfasters eager to get to the restaurant before it closes. I look around at the assembled throng as I pass through, only pausing to pick up a paper before I return to my room. Once there I shower and change then sit on the bed to read the paper. I glance at the various depressing headlines: the defence secretary resigning for breaking the ministerial code, the Bank of

England trying to keep the economy afloat and BP planning to drill for oil off Shetland - but my mind is truly occupied by my own circumstances.

I give up on the news and think about ringing Alice to ask what I should do next. Instead, I send her a text telling her about the white van and the empty house. She replies with a very un-spy-like smiley face emoji and the words 'All fine.' I think of calling her but my gut tells me that this would probably not help, my entire reason for being here feels nebulous and I am adrift in a sea of questions without answers. It is way too early to go back to Grace's house, so I decide to go and do some comfort shopping with Alice's money. I grab my phone and coat and go back out through the reception area, now empty apart from a man and woman who are in the process of checking in and a taxi waiting outside the door.

I drive to the supermarket, where I dither by the flowers. I am eventually helped with my decision by a lady in a long beige overcoat who passes by and smiles, "You in trouble then love?"

"Something like that," I reply – yes, I'm in trouble, I just don't know how deep yet. Now I have to decide if I should get some for Syd as well, or would that be too weird? In the end I leave with two bunches anyway, some replacement beers and a box of cakes, because - well, because everyone likes cake, right? I do, they have sugar.

I figure that it's now late enough to go back to the house and see what the day ahead holds.

Grace had the same idea as me. We arrive at the house within seconds of one another, me with my meagre offerings, and her with two fully loaded shopping bags and a box of beers.

"Great minds…" I say.

"And ours," Grace responds without missing a beat. It's an old thing we used to say 'back in the day'. I smile and help her carry the shopping into the house. Inside Syd is sprawled on the settee watching TV. She shouts hello and asks if there is anything she can do to help, but stops short at actually moving.

"We're fine, I'm just making some lunch, want some?"

"Maybe a bit please, I'm not that hungry."

I hand Grace her flowers, which she thanks me for and asks me to lift down a vase which she arranges them into. I take Syd hers,

"For you, I didn't want you to feel left out." She looks bemused, but thanks me and puts them on the coffee table next to her empty tea cup. I return to the kitchen and help Grace put together some sandwiches, opening and closing cupboards and drawers to locate things in the unfamiliar kitchen. By the time we are sat at the table, arranged around the puzzle, Grace has given me a complete run down of her trip to the shop; from busy checkouts where people couldn't find their purses, to the roads were everyone was 'driving like complete twats'.

"Thanks, I was driving this morning."

"I rest my case."

As we are eating Grace looks at me,

"I never asked, how's your love life?"

I snort and proceed to tell the tale of the green lizard tattoo and the spite holiday. Grace starts to giggle almost immediately.

"Matching tattoos, seriously?"

I realise that I am not going to get much in the way of sympathy here, so instead I go for self-deprecating laughs, describing the awful holiday and finishing with my dad's injury and his never-ending list of jobs. Looking back now it does have an absurd comedy to it. I finish by telling her about my sneezing fit scaring off the birds and having to travel back to the hotel with a busload of seriously pissed offed ornithologists.

We are all laughing by the end, Sydney had joined us as the show she was watching ended, evidently she had been listening from the other room, "You went on a bird watching trip?"

"It was something to do, it was awful though. I had a hangover and everyone else had binoculars and notebooks, they were quite intense. All I can tell you is there were some birds – at first."

"So it's not your new favourite hobby then?" asked Grace.

"God no, I'd rather take up train spotting, at least you can see them without a telescope."

"You could always help with my stupid jigsaw if you want a hobby. I've been at it for over a week, it's driving me bonkers."

"Well come on then, let's get it finished, you in Sydney?"

"To be honest I'd rather shit in my hands and clap. But given the vast amount of nothing there is to do I may be able to spare an hour or two. And call me Syd, I only get called Sydney by mum, usually when I'm in trouble for something."

Grace protested that this wasn't true, maybe protested a bit too much to convince me though.

We move to the table and spend the next hour looking at different shaped lugs, spaces, colours and lines. We take it in turns to make tea and choose music, with a heavy emphasis on Iggy Pop and Lou Reed – which Syd calls 'oldies', but tolerates surprisingly well. Over the music we talk about what's happened over the last couple of days, all still trying to make sense of it in our own ways. Nobody apart from me has heard from Alice today, which we agree is probably a good thing.

Grace and I indulge in some teacher talk, bemoaning the current state of education, government edicts and unaccountable OFSTED inspectors. Also, all the juicy staffroom gossip from our respective schools.

People have been leaving from both of our respective workplaces; some taking early retirement, others simply moving into different fields, tired of the constant unrealistic and unreasonable demands. I had been thinking of making a change myself, but of course I hadn't made any actual attempt to initiate that change. Mostly we focus on the way the system has been turned into an exam factory, with payments by results, run by a bunch of bean counters.

Syd has been focusing on finding the elusive pieces of a lamppost and showing little interest in the latest education act which Cameron and Clegg have presented as a universal panacea to everything that's wrong in education (it's not). She is suddenly attentive, "Say that again."

"Eh? Which bit?"

"The last bit."

"That it's all run by bureaucrats and bean counters?"

"That's it, that bit." She reverts to silence, a thoughtful look on her face.

"What is it love?" asks Grace.

"Nothing, it was just…no, nothing. Can anyone see this weird shaped bit that fits in here?"

We search for, and find, the elusive piece and the conversation moves on. I look proudly at the swathe of puzzle we have now completed, then suggest a walk and some fresh air. Grace is quick to agree, she rubs the bridge of her nose where her glasses have been sitting.

"Come on, I'll show you the way to the pub, there's a path we can walk by the canal."

"Now you're talking my language, are you coming Syd?"

"No, I ought to at least look at my uni work, just in case I ever get back to study again."

"You sure?" I ask, "Alice is paying." I hold up the card I have been given to prove it.

"No, I'm good thanks."

"Tch, youngsters today, that would never have happened back in our student days."

Grace hits me firmly on the arm.

"Ignore him, we'll see you in a bit love."

We leave the house and I let Grace guide me through the short cuts, twists and turns that lead to the black water and overgrown banks of the canal. We talk as we walk, Grace is worried for Syd, she knows she has been too wrapped up in her own problems recently and she feels powerless and scared. I try to reassure her that things will sort themselves out in the fullness of time. It feels like I am giving her platitudes, but it seems to put Grace's mind at rest for now, I guess that's one of the reasons Alice wanted me to be here.

The day is warm and pleasant, we find a quiet table outside and I collect two half pints of lager. It feels odd spending time with Grace, paying back the support and encouragement she gave me all those years ago. Odd but good, I had forgotten how at ease we were together.

As I take my first sip my phone buzzes, it is a message from Alice, '*How are things?*'

I message back,

'*your man is not discreet .*'

'*Which man?*'

'*The one in the taxi,*' I add a smiley face emoji and press send.

The phone rings almost immediately.

"Which taxi?"

"The one at the hotel, it was at the supermarket too, then again in Grace's road – you couldn't miss it with that big scrape on the wing."

"Are you sure it was the same one?"

"Well, I'm not a superspy, but I'm pretty definite, yes. Have I blown someone's cover?"

Alice's voice becomes clipped and purposeful, she is giving us orders now, "Go back to the house, right now. Don't stop on the way. Call Sydney and tell her to lock the door, don't do anything until Carl gets there."

"Why? Is it…"

"Go back to the house now."

The call ends abruptly, I look at Grace who's been listening in to the conversation. Her face is ashen.

"Is Syd safe?"

"I'm sure she is, come on we'd better go."

We leave our beer undrunk and start walking briskly back, half running. Grace becomes more agitated as she tries and fails to reach Syd on the phone. We retrace our steps, no conversation now, just motion. We go back through the short cuts and alleys to Grace's house, which stares blankly at us as we approach. Now Grace does run, I follow with a sick, empty feeling in my stomach. Muffled sounds from inside reveal themselves to be Dave Grohl at full volume as Grace opens the door and hurries inside. I hold back slightly and arrive as the sound is being turned down and Syd is asking, "Why wouldn't I be alright?"

Before Grace has chance to answer a voice behind me asks if everyone is okay. It's Carl, standing in the hallway, the door open behind him. Not the affable, easy-going Carl who had been ferrying us around for the last couple of days though. This Carl is dressed in black and is all business, he looks different, alert, serious.

"We're fine," I tell him.

"Good, tell the ladies to grab what they need, a small bag each, and be outside asap."

He does not elaborate on this, it is given as a direct and unarguable instruction. He stands in the open doorway scanning the street and waiting for me to follow his orders, which I do. I relay his message to Grace and Syd who also do not question it. They disappear upstairs and the sound of drawers opening and closing and footsteps on the landing drift down to me. Syd reappears first, followed closely by Grace.

"What's going on?" asks Syd.

"I don't know, but Carl wants us to go now."

I point to the open doorway that Carl has just vacated and we all move towards it.

Syd

Finally the door closed and she had the house to herself. It was not that he didn't seem nice, and it was good to see Mum happy for a change, but a bit of time on her own would be good right now. She rifled through the CD collection looking for something from this century and eventually settles on the new Foo Fighters album. Making sure it is put on loud enough for the sound to fill the house, she sat at the table with her text books open around her, resting on the incomplete jigsaw.

The whole time something niggled in the back of her mind, like an itch she couldn't scratch. It was something to do with what they had been saying, but she couldn't quite put her finger on what it was.

She was lost in the world of the 19th century realists, absorbed in the world of Millet and Courbet, when the door burst open and Grace came rushing in, shouting over the music to ask if she was alright.

"Why wouldn't I be alright?" she asked back, lowering her voice mid-sentence as the music was turned down low.

"Nothing, just checking."

"You've only been gone half an hour, don't I get any peace?"

"I'm not sure I'd call this peace."

"You know what I mean, anyway why wouldn't I be alright? And why are you back so quick?"

Before she gets an answer to this there are voices at the door, and an instruction to pack a bag and meet outside as quickly as possible is shouted to them, essentials only.

"Why?"

"Because Carl said, he seems pretty wired."

"Carl the driver?"

"Yes, that Carl – he's waiting for us."

Syd and Grace got the tone of voice and went upstairs to throw together the things they thought they might need. This does not take long for Syd as most of her stuff is still at her flat waiting to be collected. She grabs a phone charger, hair scrunchies, a brush and some of her older underwear and t-shirts that she had not taken with her when she went to uni. She crams it into her old school backpack and meets her mum, with a battered blue holdall, on the landing.

"What's happened?"

"I don't know exactly, I'll ask Carl."

Syd looked back into her room, grabbed a baggy old stripy sweater from the back of the door then hurried downstairs to the open front door. Carl is in the garden, looking up and down the close.

"Good, everybody got everything, we can pick up more supplies later if we need to. I'm going out to the car, wait here until you hear the engine running then come out and join me. Make sure to buckle up. Everyone clear?"

He waited for them all to nod then jogged calmly towards the same blue car they had arrived in. Syd watched the incongruous sight of a man in black getting into a family car, if this was a film it would be a Range Rover she thought. But it isn't a film, she dutifully waited for the engine to start and began to move forward. Before any of them can take a full step the car lurched backwards, crushing the shrubs and flowers on its way to the front lawn, and stopping abruptly in front of them.

Slightly nervous now, they hurried into the car and Syd found her seat belt. Before she could fasten it the car shot forward again, back over the flower beds, wheels spinning and engine roaring. They bounced onto the road and accelerated towards the junction, where they joined the traffic on the main road without slowing. Syd looked behind, but could not see what they were fleeing from, only a taxi pulling away from outside number 11 – the Grants' house. She looked ahead to see that Carl was squeezing the car past other vehicles, flashing his lights and fitting through improbably small-looking spaces. The engine revved and roared as Carl ignored all rules of the road - and basic common sense - as he single-mindedly put as much distance as he could between them and whatever or whoever it was they were running from.

Alice

Shit!

Alice knew something had gone wrong the moment he started talking about the taxi. As soon as she ended the call she contacted Carl. There was an extraction plan in place, several in fact, she told Carl it was Plan A. He did not need anything else, he simply answered 'yes, Ma'am,' and hung up.

Now she had to wait for Carl to message back and let her know if things had gone smoothly. While she waited she contacted friends and colleagues in other centres, to check nobody else had somehow become involved without her knowledge. Her suspicion that none had was quickly confirmed, so if not them, who?

The Americans had not contacted her, and if she approached them they would know immediately that something was up – if they didn't already. She asked one of the tech guys in the basement to listen out for any noise that might give her a clue, then got Mrs Baker to arrange her transport.

Whatever was happening, and she had a good idea what it was, would not happen without her being in control of the situation. She wondered again if sending Sydney home had been the best idea, although she knew it had been their only viable plan at the time.

Her phone rang, it was Carl, calm as always, "Safely en-route to destination, no escorts."

"Thanks Carl, see you there."

At least they were keeping one step ahead – for now. She sat, pensive, as she waited for Mrs Baker to let her know when the helicopter had arrived.

A message appeared in the corner of her computer screen. Not Carl, but Sarah, the operative who had been keeping eyes on the house. It simply stated '*subjects clear.*' Alice called her to get a fuller update on the current status.

Sarah had been keeping watch from the van, Carl had left to shadow two of the subjects as they had gone off for an afternoon walk. Sarah had remained at the house with the girl. When Carl had called and given the order to evacuate she had followed protocol, keeping the van engine running, eyes on the road and ready to assist when needed – standard operating procedure.

The couple had returned and Carl, close behind them, told her they were initiating the evacuation now. He radioed this as he backed his car up to the house, adding 'block that fucking taxi' as he herded everybody into the car. Sarah looked and saw a minicab pulling out from behind a low hedge a few houses up and wondered how she hadn't spotted it earlier, although she could see that it had parked strategically at an angle that would not have been visible from where she was, but even so... As Carl sped off Sarah pulled the van diagonally across the road in his wake.

The taxi screeched to a halt, then reversed at speed before accelerating towards her, swerving over the curb and crossing two neighbouring gardens, spreading a mess of plants and carefully tended lawns behind it and dragging a rose bush along the road on its exhaust.

Carl was already gone, she thought she might have held the taxi up for long enough. She had tried to tail the taxi, but had quickly lost it. The van was great for stake outs, but crap for pursuits.

Alice mulled this information over. This had definitely upped the stakes. The vague description she had of the driver - short fair hair, Caucasian, male - was very little to go on. She hoped the tech guys might get more from traffic cameras, but was not hugely optimistic about this. For now they were going to the next level of preparedness.

CHAPTER 9
Escape

Carl has slowed down now, he is driving at the speed limit and obeying all the rules of the road. I can see him checking his mirrors frequently as he drives away from the town, not taking a direct route, but ducking and diving down side roads and through residential areas. He makes a brief phone call before we get onto the motorway and start our unexpected journey, heading north. The houses and shops dwindle away and are replaced with utilitarian office blocks and warehouses, which in turn give way to fields and areas of woodland that stand back from the barriers that line the edge of the road.

Carl is still keeping his eyes on the road behind us, alternately slowing down and speeding up, ducking behind large lorries and changing lanes frequently when they approach junctions. He is all business, although the further we go the more he appears to relax. His responses to questions about their destination are, as expected, non-committal.

Grace has got shotgun and I am in the back with Syd. She asks me what is going on and I tell her what I know, which amounts to a whole lot of not much. She then sits quietly, staring out of the window. I look at her, trying not to be too obvious, and am taken again with how much she looks like Grace at her age, I find it both disconcerting and exciting. I know that this is not the best time, the worst possible time perhaps, but I realise that I never stopped loving Grace. I had been so wrapped-up in such a toxic mixture of self-loathing and self-preservation, that I had been incapable of seeing what I had.

My maudlin reverie is interrupted by Grace. She turns around and asks if I'm okay, or –more likely – if Syd is okay. We both answer that we're fine and Grace immediately responds with a question about food and drink. She is asking if either of us managed to pick up anything from the house on the way out. Of course, we didn't. She now turns to Carl and tells him we'll need to stop and get something at the next services. I'm glad, as I need to pee, but didn't want to be the one who suggested we take a break from escaping.

"No problem," Carl replies, "it's coming up in 6 or 7 miles."

It's a relief, I can hold on for that long. It's also a relief that Carl is okay with it, we seem to have stepped down from Defcon 1 now we have some miles behind us. He is still alert and attentive as we pull into the services and park up in a far corner, next to a black Audi. We make a beeline for the building, Syd and Grace turn into the shop while I carry on to the toilets.

I wait for them by the door and we walk together back to the car.

"You okay?" I ask Grace.

"Not really, any idea where we're going?"

"Not a clue, apart from North."

"I'd worked that out already, anyway, you think everywhere's North," she replies sarcastically.

"It is from where I live."

"He's quite the action man isn't he?" she indicates Carl, who is still finishing his phone call.

"Yeah, I'm glad he's on our side."

"Is he? Whose side are we on then?"

I admit that I don't really know, I'm still a little unsure how the events of the last few days have led me to where I am now. I have no idea what's going on, or how it might end up. I sense Grace's unease. No, make that fear - it is in her face, the way her mouth twists and her brow furrows. It is in the way she is walking, arms wrapped around herself and looking around compulsively at every sound and movement. I think I am probably showing some of the same signs of hyper-vigilance myself. In the car Sydney had been attacking her fingernails with renewed vigour and twisting locks of her hair. Grace asks if I think it will be okay, I give her the best answer I can, "I think it will be fine, Alice knows what she's doing."

Grace stops abruptly, I take another step before I realise she isn't with me, then turn around, facing her. She steps forward and wraps her arms around me, putting her head against my chest. I put my own arms around her as she looks up and says, "Whatever it is, I'm glad you're here. I wouldn't want to be doing this by myself, and I've missed you."

"I've missed you too," I reply. I can smell shampoo in her hair, maybe something citrussy, and I feel the warmth of her against me. I realise the truth of my last statement now I have said it out loud. The mood is broken as Syd catches up then passes us, "Get a room you two."

She walks on without looking back, taking another bite from her chocolate bar as she finishes speaking. The moment helps dispel some of the anxiety we had been carrying, in a moment of normality we step apart, laughing, then continue walking towards the car where Carl is talking on the phone. He stops talking for long enough to direct us to get into the Audi rather than the Ford, so parking next to it had not been a coincidence, just another piece of an elaborately prepared plan.

In the car Syd changes place with Grace. The new car is bigger and more comfortable than the Ford, with leather seats and more leg space, which I am grateful for.

"I thought you two would want to sit next to each other," she says as she closes her door, a hint of playful sarcasm in her voice.

Carl has one last look around the half empty parking area. Apparently satisfied with what he sees, he gets in and starts the car.

As we pull away I feel Grace slip her hand into mine and I hold it tight.

"Settle down," he tells us, "we've got quite a long drive ahead. You can relax a bit, nobody has followed us, but keep your phones off in case they have access to the relay towers."

We obediently take our phones out and ensure they are switched off as the car builds up speed and joins the fast moving motorway traffic, heading inexorably towards our unknown destination.

Alice

The farmhouse sits alone in a sea of fields, its brickwork is encrusted with trails of ivy that flow up from amongst the weeds of the cracked and broken concrete of the courtyard. Outbuildings and barns gather around the main building in a protective cordon. Where they had once been utilitarian and convenient, they are now dilapidated and tired. The late afternoon sun is casting a pool of light amidst the dark shadows that creep from the paint-peeling doorways and a blackbird dashes from the roof of the barn to settle on the shining silver of the phone wire.

Alice sits in the Volvo with the door open, listening to the engine quietly click and cool. She is looking at the blank screen of her phone, which she abruptly shoves into her pocket as she mutters 'bollocks'. Only the blackbird is listening, and he seems indifferent.

Getting out of the car she takes a deep breath, then goes into the darkened doorway of the farmhouse. She disappears into the shadows before the door closes behind her.

Inside everything is functional and clean, nothing you would describe as fancy, apart from the elaborate encrypted router that sits blinking in a corner of the kitchen counter. She gets a glass of water and sits at the table to wait. She knows she may need to share what she has found out, but is worried that it has made things more complicated. She certainly doesn't want to alarm or scare Sydney and the others any more than they are already.

The taxi had been quickly located, abandoned in a car park at a shopping centre on the edge of town. It had been thoroughly wiped down, so no prints, but some things can't be easily removed. The forensic team had been assiduous in their work, as always. They had found traces of gunshot residue on the back of the steering wheel. The fact that the pursuer is probably armed puts things on another footing. Carl and the team have now been authorised to use live rounds.

Still, she has never shied away from or delegated the difficult parts of her job before, and she's not going to start today. In the years since she took over at the centre she has had to make some tough decisions, choices that have impacted on other people. She is as sure as she can be that her judgement has always been good.

Sometimes this had meant people lost their liberty, sometimes they got a second chance. Frequently it had meant dealing with people she would really rather not deal with. The Americans were improving now Obama was president, but there was still the lingering paranoia of the Bush administration, along with the ongoing conflict in Afghanistan and the continuing fallout from 9/11 that made things more complicated and confrontational.

As for Syd, there was no way she was going to let an innocent young girl who got caught in the wrong place at the wrong time, take the fall. Not on her watch.

CHAPTER 10
Farm

I am not used to sitting in the back of cars, the twists and turns of

the country lanes have conspired to make me feel queasy. I am hoping we will arrive at our destination sometime soon. I lost track of our location some time back, after we left the motorway and started to weave through smaller roads and lanes – some so narrow and unused we barely fit between the hedgerows; grass and weeds form an optimistic green stripe down the centre as they try to reclaim the space as their own.

It is a long time since we passed any towns or villages, the alien names on the signposts hold no meaning for me and give no insights to our location. Conversation in the car has dwindled to nothing, so we look out of our respective windows as Carl ferries us to wherever it is we are going.

Eventually we come to a halt. Carl gets out and opens a gate , recessed and overgrown that it would be easy to miss it altogether. The weatherworn gate has the words 'The Farm' carved into the wood, still legible in spite of the covering of lichen. We drive onto a rough track and Carl stops again as he gets out to resecure the gate.

"I guess we're nearly there then?" says Grace.

"Where?" asks Syd.

"Here, The Farm, wherever it is. I suppose we'll find out soon," I answer.

After the miles travelled, this last stretch along the uneven approach to our destination, feels unfeasibly long. Eventually we turn a sharp bend that reveals a small farmhouse with some outbuildings, appearing from behind some ancient trees. A mud-spattered Volvo sits alone in the courtyard and light glows in the gathering gloom from a single lit window on the lower floor. The door next to the window opens as I decamp from the car, stretching my legs and back, along with the obligatory accompanying middle-aged grunting sound effects. Alice steps out to greet us from the shadow of the doorway.

We are directed inside and given directions to the toilet, the recently boiled kettle is put to task, and Alice busies herself – waiting until we are all together before we talk. Carl speaks briefly to her before he goes back outside, takes a backpack from the boot of the car and disappears back in the direction we came from, on foot this time. Finally we assemble in the kitchen, chairs scraping on the stone floor as we sit at the large wooden table, scarred and dented from years of hard work, and with steaming mugs of tea and coffee in front of us.

Carl returns, apparently satisfied for now, he nods at Alice then collects the tea that has been left for him and leans against the counter facing us.

"What's going on?" asks Grace, "Are you going to tell us?"

"Not just yet," answers Alice. She leaves the building and we hear the sound of a car boot opening and closing. Syd and Grace both look at me, and I shrug. Alice returns directly with a large insulated container which she puts on the worktop and opens.

"I hope Chinese is okay, I took the liberty of bringing a selection, so there should be something for everyone. Sorry if it's not hot, but this should have at least kept it warm."

She then proceeds to lift out container after container of food. It looks as though she might have just ordered one of everything from the menu. There was no need for an apology either, the food is still warm, the aromas fill the room and I realise how long it is since I had anything apart from snacks. It appears to be the same for everyone as Grace finds a selection of mismatched bowls in a cupboard and we all start filling them with noodles, rice and anything else that takes our fancy from our private buffet.

The conversation focusses on what is what in the various foil dishes for now. 'Who likes what?', 'Please can you pass?' and 'Have you tried?' It transpires that the incongruously modern silver fridge has recently been stocked with beers which are shared around. Carl sticks to tap water. Along with Alice he has unwrapped some chopsticks from the food order, they are both using them proficiently. Grace, Syd and I have all opted for more familiar cutlery.

Alice pauses and speaks to us.

"I do hope you'll bear with me," she says, "I will try and explain, but I thought it would be easier for all of us if we are fed, watered and comfortable first. So, tuck in and enjoy." She raises her bottle of beer in a toast and we do as we are told, eating our fill.

The leftovers seem to be as much again as the food we have eaten. They are loaded into the fridge as we tidy away the detritus from our feast and clear the table, leaving only the active beer bottles and a handful of fortune cookies. I wonder what they would tell us if we weren't too bloated to open them, I somehow doubt that they would be able to capture the zeitgeist in the farmhouse kitchen. There is little conversation and the room is filled with nervous energy and anticipation. Carl excuses himself,

"I'll check the perimeter Ma'am." He goes outside; presumably he already knows what we are about to be told. Eventually, when we are sat back at the table, Alice appears thoughtful and there is a moment of absolute silence as we wait for her to start. When she does her tone is almost conversational, she smiles, gives a little shake of her head and says, "Well, it's been a busy summer that's for sure. I'm certain it won't surprise you that the NSA – America's National Security Agency – have been gathering information and intelligence about everybody, at home and abroad. Not just them though, GCHQ have been poking and prying too, along with every other major player on the planet.

I couldn't give you any details, even if I had them. But there are worries that sooner or later someone is going to blow the whole thing out of the water any time now, all of their dirty secrets and underhand dealings – every shitty thing they've done to each other, and to everyone else, for the last five years. Our dirty laundry too come to that, I'm not proud to say we've done our own share of shady business. I don't know why they think Sydney is so important, but I intend to get to the bottom of it. Our intel thinks they are more likely to be exposed by an insider who is disillusioned, another Bradley Manning spilling the beans on Wikileaks, but the Americans are positive that the threat lies abroad. It's why they are so concerned about the hack."

I am not convinced that Alice knows as little as she is pretending, but I get the point. I can see how this would make Syd very interesting to them. Alice continues, "The Americans are not communicating with us and won't tell us what might, or might not, have been taken in the hack, they're not even admitting it has happened officially. But my sources tell me that whatever it is, they are extremely keen to see that it doesn't come into the public domain. Personally, I think it's a lost cause, sooner or later people will know. But until then they will do whatever they can to try and put a gag on it."

A collective cloud of thoughts hangs over us, then Syd asks quietly, "So, they still think I have something?"

"They're definitely worried that you might, yes. I'm sure you don't, we know who most likely does, so we've got some bargaining power here. I think we can work something out, but I'm worried about how they found you so quickly and easily. In fact, how they even knew to look for you."

"What do you mean?" asked Syd.

"I mean, nobody outside of our service, and even then not everybody, knew about you. As far as I know none of the other agencies were even close, we thought we'd closed it down."

"So somebody told them?" I ask.

"It's possible, right now we need to sit tight. This is a safe house, nobody knows we are here, Carl and I are going to be your best friends for a while I'm afraid."

"How long?" asks Syd.

"Piece of string long," replies Alice, "sorry, I really don't know. There's a lot going on behind the scenes right now." She looks at us apologetically with half a shrug, then stands up and goes to fill the kettle. "Anyone need a coffee? I'm afraid there's only instant, I must get a coffee machine put in here, but it'll do for now."

Syd

Syd is feeling more and more like the unwilling star of an improvised film, it is not a good feeling. Everything is happening so fast, events piling up on top of events and any façade of normality abandoned. She wonders if this is what being grown-up is like, having little or no control over events which should be held in check by a responsible adult. She knows that the 'adults' are trying their best, and she is happy to defer the decision making to them for now. But her mum looks worried, and even the woman, Alice, seems to have lost some of her composure.

There is something else, something that is still niggling at her, trying to convince her of its importance. She still can't quite grasp it, she thought the long drive would be enough time to work it out – but apparently it wasn't.

She looks around the kitchen, apart from the fridge and the black box with the flashing lights everything is old and well-used. Scratched, worn, lovingly polished, it looks like a film set, although the present company make for an unlikely looking cast.

Mum has an intense and slightly glazed expression, although she has looked like that quite a lot in the last year, since dad left - or 'fucked off with his floozy' as she liked to think of it. To be fair she had met Dad's new partner a couple of times, although she did seem quite nice – for a marriage wrecker - they both knew they were never going to be friends. Mum seemed to exist in baggy jumpers and jeans now, she would regularly lapse into quiet moments of melancholy that Syd didn't know how to respond to. Last Christmas had been shit; the two of them, a small nut roast and some token decorations. After they had opened each other's presents, Mum had gone upstairs 'for a rest', from where Syd could hear her quietly sobbing. She had put on some music to drown it out, because underneath her anger, she had felt like sobbing too.

The reappearance of Mum's ex from college had been the first time for a long time that Syd had seen a glimpse of mum's old self. Once she had gotten over her initial anger his appearance triggered, she clearly welcomed his presence and was happy he was around. He was nice, although she still didn't fully understand the whole reason of why they split up, but she definitely got the gist of it yesterday. She just didn't quite get why one or other of them couldn't have just moved.

After he told them his story yesterday she had seen mum's eyes glistening, and had realised that this had been something mum had needed to hear, had waited a long time for. He, in turn, had seemed relieved to finally explain what had happened to him. He had been hesitant and cautious at first, but now appeared more relaxed. A weight had been lifted from him and she could see him gradually becoming as comfortable as any of them were in this shitty situation.

He was sitting across the table from her now, for someone in his 40's he hadn't let himself go too badly, like some older men do. He was wearing worn DM's, faded jeans and a baggy old Nike sweatshirt, his hair was starting to grey but was mostly still all there. She supposed Mum could do a lot worse. Also, he smiled a lot and had not patronised her, she appreciated both those things.

Alice reminded her of Judi Dench in that James Bond film dad had taken her to a couple of years ago, mostly because he had wanted to go. She didn't really look that much like her, for a start her hair was too long, and she was younger. But she was sharp – everything about her said 'don't mess with me'- in a favourite teacher kind of way. She thought that if she could see inside her head it would be the equivalent of a human supercomputer, whizzing and whirring with possibilities and probabilities. It was clear she had been the one responsible for the plotting and planning of their escape and keeping them safe from…. well, from whatever it was she was keeping them safe from.

Closer to her age, Carl had undergone a transformation in the last twelve hours. He seemed nice, although not her type, initially she had thought he was just a driver. Now he had turned into more of a bodyguard/action-hero. He had gone back outside again, slipping away into the dark. She wasn't certain, but she thought the slight bulge at his hip might be a gun, she wondered again how deep the shit she was in really was.

She had checked out the bedroom situation earlier, when she had gone upstairs to use the bathroom.

"There are only two bedrooms," she announced as the conversation dwindled. Everyone looked at her and she repeated, "There are only two bedrooms. I'm tired and want to go to bed, but I don't know where we're all going to sleep. There are five of us." She added the last in case anybody had not understood the significance of her earlier statement.

Alice replied, "Carl won't need a bed, he'll be working. I'll be okay down here, I've got things I need to do. That leaves one each for you guys and the settee, there are piles of blankets in the cupboard on the landing."

"Okay, I'm off to bed then," Syd answers, and disappears upstairs. She has already decided the small back bedroom is hers.

CHAPTER 11
Wake-up call

There is a moment of silence while Grace and Alice finish their respective mugs of coffee, mine is long gone. Grace asks Alice, "Are we safe here?"

"I can't think of anywhere safer, except maybe the centre. But until I know where information is leaking from I want to keep Syd's location as private as I possibly can."

I find it hard to believe that the centre may not be safe, but I'm glad we're here not there. I move from the table, holding up the crumpled packet of cigarettes I have pulled from my pocket, to indicate my intention.

"Don't go too far from the building," I am instructed.

I don't ask why, I hadn't been intending to anyway. I stand outside the door in the small pool of yellow light cascading from the kitchen window. I look in and see Grace and Alice talking intensely. I jump slightly when Carl appears from the shadows at my side and puts his hand on my arm, I hadn't heard him approach.

"Everything okay?" he asks.

"Uh, yes thanks. You?"

"It's all quiet, so it's all good. That was a good spot with the taxi before, none of us had clocked it, well done."

He claps me on the shoulder, making me rock forward slightly, then vanishes into the shadows again before I have chance to answer – or ask him anything. Our short exchange had raised questions for me:

Was he expecting it to not be quiet?

How many people had 'not clocked' the taxi?

How many people were here now?

What was his job exactly?

I decide that maybe I don't want the answers to my unasked questions. I take the compliment with a certain amount of smugness, extinguish my cigarette and go back inside.

Alice is still at the table, laptop open in front of her. She gives me a nod as I close the door. Grace is rinsing her mug in the sink. She wipes it on the towel and tells me she is tired and is going to turn in.

"I'll take the settee then?" I frown at the lumpy old couch through the door to the next room, it doesn't look I'll be getting a great deal of sleep. Grace looks into the room, then turns to me,

"If you really want to, it doesn't look that comfortable, you'd get no sleep and a backache. The front bedroom has a double bed, we can share – if you don't mind that is."

I can't think why I would mind, it's not like we hadn't shared a bed before after all. Of course, back in the day it was single beds and we didn't sleep much. When we did it was the deep and undisturbed sleep that only young people can truly manage. It's also not like Grace isn't an attractive woman. As usual I'm having trouble with the signals – is Grace asking me to 'share' the bed, or 'share the bed'? I don't know, adulting is still hard sometimes, even after all the years of practise I've had. I make up my mind that this is not a 'sharing the bed' scenario.

"You're probably right about the settee. I'll just dry up the mugs while you get changed if you want."

"Ooh, Mr Domesticated! Knock yourself out, I'll see you in a minute."

I take my time, I glance back at Alice as I finish, "Goodnight."

"Sleep well," she tells me, smiling. She continues to smile as she looks back down to her laptop and I go to the stairs. When I get to the room Grace is getting into bed. She has stripped down to her tee shirt and pants and is just sliding under the faded patchwork quilt.

"No pyjamas, why does everybody forget to pack pyjamas when they pack in a hurry?" she says with a smile.

If by 'pack in a hurry' she means 'make an emergency exit from a house, running from unknown assailants, in the shortest possible time', I don't think it's all that surprising to be honest.

"All my stuff's back at the hotel still." I strip down to my tee shirt and boxers and climb into the bed. "I'm sure we'll be able to get some fresh clothes soon, from somewhere. I'll ask Alice tomorrow. I need some clean underwear."

"You can borrow a pair of mine."

"Thank you, I'll bear it in mind."

"You're welcome. Switch the light off and snuggle over here, I'm chilly."

I obediently follow her instructions and find her in the dark, lying on her side with her back to me. I put one arm over her and our mutual warmth joins forces to start heating up the bed. This feels wrong and right at the same time, I feel the smoothness of her skin and the softness of her flesh and enjoy it.

"I feel safe like this, thank you."

"It's my pleasure."

"Do you remember the first time we shared a bed?"

She is talking about the time we spent together after the Halloween party, after I had been moved to my new college by Alice and her boss.

"You made me miss a lecture."

"A seminar actually, you missed the lecture all by yourself."

"Whatever, anyway, yes I do remember."

How could I forget, Grace had been my salvation when I had been at my lowest point, I try to remember what she had done and said that had helped me through a difficult time in my life, so I can repay her kindness. I squeeze her gently, "We were good together though, weren't we?"

"We were, they were good times." She reaches and puts her own hand on top of mine, "I'm glad you're here."

"Me too."

I feel her relax and I lie still as she slips into sleep. If I could bottle this moment and keep it forever I would, but in spite of my determination to savour every minute I too start to sink into sleep.

*

There's a word for this; 'discombobulated'. Right now, I'm not entirely sure where I am or how I got here, everything is unfamiliar. It only lasts a few seconds, but if you had asked me in this particular moment what my name is, I would probably have had to pass.

I had been dreaming, something to do with a beach in Greece. I had been walking, very quickly, away from a tattoo artist. A lone figure had appeared at the end of the beach, as I approached they started to call to me.

"Mum, wake up Mum, it's important."

The voice is insistent and demanding, I am confused as to why they are calling me mum.

Then everything clicks into place. Syd is standing over Grace gently nudging her shoulder. Grace looks as confused as me for a moment, then sits up alert and concerned, "What is it Syd?"

"I've remembered something."

"Can't it wait until the morning?"

I look at my watch, we have barely been asleep for an hour. Syd is now perched on the end of the bed and Grace is sitting up, hair tousled and crumpled, but awake and alert.

"I've remembered something, I think it might be important. I might know where he lives"

"Who?"

"Rick, of course."

As we process this, Alice's voice comes from the bedroom doorway, "Hold on to your thoughts. I'm putting the kettle on, you can tell us what you've remembered, then we'll decide if it is important or not." She looks impeccable, as if she has had a full night of refreshing sleep. (Maybe she has slept, I doubt it somehow.) She has got a thick, warm-looking cardigan on over her work clothes – at least one of us packed properly! She leaves the room and Syd goes with her while Grace and I put on jeans and sweatshirts and follow them to the kitchen.

We join them at the table where there are already mugs out and the kettle is well on its way to boiling. I feel the chill of the night now, the cold stone floor on my bare feet under the table, in the shadow of the bright kitchen light. Syd gets the milk, I have no idea what she needs to tell us, but the look on her face tells me that she thinks it matters; lips pursed, a distant look in her eyes as she mentally rehearses what she wants to say. Clearly, she believes it's important, so one way or another I guess it is.

Finally, we gather around the table. I wrap my hands around the hot mug in front of me and look around the faces of the women surrounding me, waiting for someone to start. Alice breaks the silence, "Sydney, I want you tell me what it is you've remembered. Tell it all and tell it slowly. Try not to leave out anything, however small, sometimes the devil is in the details."

Syd takes a sip of her drink then looks at Grace before turning her eyes to Alice, "It may not be anything, I'm sorry I woke you all up."

"It's okay, we need anything we can get right now."

"Well," continued Syd, "it was something you two said." She looks from Grace to me. "Then you," she looks back to Alice, "said you needed a coffee machine here, and I couldn't put my finger on it at first. But I just woke up and it was there, I remembered it."

I slurp my tea, I am wide awake now, and even more intrigued than before. I see Grace and Alice have both lent imperceptibly forward. We all clutch our mugs and nobody interrupts.

"I'd arranged to meet Rick at my place one afternoon, on my way back I stopped at the little coffee place near my flat. He likes his coffee, really bloody fussy about it. Anyway, it's a nice coffee shop, a little family run place, not one of those big chains. Plus, they only use Fairtrade. I thought it would be good to have some fresh coffee. Rick was there when I got home, after I finished drinking mine I said how nice it was. Rick said 'Yep, it sure is – not as good as the Bean Counter though'."

She stops and looks around us expectantly. I stare blankly back, not getting it at all. Alice is several steps ahead of me of course.

"So, you think that's somewhere he goes regularly?"

Now the penny drops for me, the Bean Counter is the name of a coffee shop. I recall the conversation Grace and I had when one or other of us had used the phrase.

"Yes, he's really funny about coffee, he insists on starting the day with good coffee, says he can't function otherwise."

"But there must be hundreds of coffee shops called the Bean Counter," I say.

"I thought so too," replied Syd, "but I guess it's too obvious. I Googled it, there are only four or five. Plus, after he said that he said 'best coffee North of Watford'. He said it under his breath, more to himself than me, but I heard it clearly. So that narrows it down to just two that I can find, one in Liverpool and one in Coventry."

Alice looks thoughtful, "So, that could be where we'll find him?"

"Maybe, he likes his coffee, and you don't have a favourite coffee place that you've only been to once or twice, do you?"

Alice sips her coffee and says nothing, the rest of us wait for her. Grace looks as though she is about to speak when Alice abruptly stands up.

"Sydney, that could be the best thing that's happened today, it's always better to have something than nothing. Find those two shops for me again."

She opens the laptop that had been sitting on the table and types in an improbably long password before turning it to face Syd. She then walks to the door and summons Carl. By the time he is in the kitchen Syd has found the required pages.

"Okay, me and Carl need to talk, can you all give us a minute?"

We all obediently shuffle into the sitting room, the exposed beams throw shadows across the ceiling from the dim wall lamps. I sit on the sofa with Grace, Syd sits opposite, disappearing as the oversized armchair swallows her. She is brighter now, smiling in spite of the fact that it is the middle of the night. She looks between us and grins, "I know I told you two to get a room, I didn't think you'd take it literally."

"Syd," Grace reprimands, "it's not like that, okay?"

"I don't care if it is, you two oldies deserve some fun."

"Syd!" again, the tone is not severe.

I am not sure what I object to most - being accused of acts of impropriety with someone's mother, or being called an 'oldie'. I feel I should back Grace up, but before I get a chance she speaks again, quietly.

"We've known each other for a long time. I miss your dad, and it's nice having someone to share things with, even if it is in these awful circumstances."

I feel her hand reaching for mine and take it, warm and soft, giving my hand a gentle squeeze. Syd levers herself from the depths of the chair and wedges herself between the arm of the sofa and Grace, causing Grace to press up against me. Syd hugs Grace, "I'm sorry mum, I was only teasing. I'm really sorry I got us all into this."

My hand is released as Grace returns the hug.

"It's okay, don't apologise for something that wasn't your fault. You did well tonight, I'm sure this will all get sorted out. We'll do it together, all of us."

She looks at me and I nod and try to look reassuring. But when I open my mouth the only thing that comes out is, "Oldies?!"

*

Before long Alice gets back to us, "Go back to bed, get some sleep. We'll be leaving early tomorrow."

"How early?" Syd asks.

"Early, early. It's okay, you can sleep in the car."

"We're going to find the Bean Counter aren't we?" I ask.

"Yes, big day ahead, go back to bed, I'll give you a call in the morning."

We obediently climb back up the creaky stairs to return to our rooms.

I'm glad to get back under the duvet. It's cold again now, but not as cold as it was downstairs. Grace gets back in and slides over to me, pushing herself close.

"Warm me up, I'm freezing."

"Me too, get your cold feet off of me."

"No way, not until I'm warmed up."

She leans and kisses my cheek. The kiss is interrupted as she opens her mouth wide and yawns.

"Early start then?" I say, "Is it even worth going to sleep?"

"I'm getting my beauty sleep, I need it." Grace pulls the duvet to her side of the bed and wraps herself in it.

"You don't need it, you look great."

"Schmooze – go to sleep."

I don't think I will, but it's late and the day has taken its toll, I soon find myself wandering empty, echoing, endless corridors, sometimes I am in The Centre, sometimes I am back at college. Grace, Syd, Alice and Lisa keep disappearing around the shadows of distant unreachable corners.

Alice

It could be something, or it could be nothing. Whichever it is, it can't hurt to look into it. Alice knows she can't go through the normal channels. She doesn't know what went wrong before, but the Americans are getting information from somewhere. She has no idea how, but until the leak is plugged it's down to her and Carl, and each of their own most trusted contacts.

She recounted the new information that Syd has supplied them with to Carl, then she waited for his response. Of course, she is his superior, but she was keen to know what he would say. Her suspicion was that he would come up with an outline of a plan broadly similar – if not the same - as the one she was considering. She had worked with him for several years, long enough to know she could trust his judgement – and his loyalty.

He takes his time; she knows he is running through myriad options and scenarios. She also knows he is aware that they are on their own for now, he would have realised that the moment he got the evacuate order. This pre-arranged rendezvous point at the farmhouse is a secret failsafe that only a tiny number of people know about, it's the last resort when things have gone badly wrong.

The farm used to belong to her grandparents, she had enjoyed many summers here as a child, helping Grandad Jim with chores and following Nana Mary around, talking to her as she fed the animals and prepared the meals. It was a proper working farm then, with men coming and going and all the smells and noises associated with the animals and harvests. Her happy, carefree summers had been idyllic in her memory. She had inherited the farm when her grandparents had died; first Nana Mary, closely followed by Grandad Jim, and found she had not been able to let it go. The fields were all rented to neighbouring farmers now, for a peppercorn rent. The closest neighbour paid the rent in kind, by looking after the farmhouse and making sure it was in good repair for when she needed a place to retreat, rest and think. It was her private place and was not listed as her residence on the work database, she had only shared its existence with one or two people who might need to find her in an emergency. Carl was one of those people.

Carl finishes his cogitations, "I'll go to Liverpool then?"

Alice feels her faith in him is vindicated; he has second guessed her next step.

"Yes, leave at first light. We'll go to Coventry; I want to keep them all together. You've got the pictures, haven't you?"

There are a handful of grainy, low-resolution images of Rick taken from security cameras. Mostly he had been adept at avoiding them, covering his face with a baseball cap and keeping his back to their prying lenses. There were some profile shots and a fuzzy full-face image. They weren't much, but would hopefully be good enough to make an ID if necessary.

"Yes, Ma'am, I'll be ready to leave at sunup. That should get me there before it opens, and then I can have eyes on it all day."

"Okay, we won't be leaving too long after you, we'll set up shop in Coventry. What's your money on?"

"I think Liverpool is the most likely, but I'm not really convinced about either – it's a long shot."

"It is, but I'd rather be doing something apart from sitting around waiting. Stay low, and only contact me if it's necessary."

"Yes, Ma'am."

He goes back out into the night to resume his watchful vigil, Alice wishes he wouldn't call her Ma'am, but she knows his background and that it's not a habit he will easily break. She goes to the sitting room to tell the others what the plan is, as she opens the door she is greeted with laughter as they all share a joke. They are all scrunched up on the settee together, a picture of familial harmony; it suits them. She explains the plan and suggests they all might want to get some sleep as they've got an early start, then watches as they all go unquestioningly back up the stairs to their rooms.

Returning to the kitchen she makes another coffee and starts to make phone calls in preparation for tomorrow. She knows there have been too many late nights recently, that her body will need to take some time to recover and reset when this is over. She promises herself that once things have quietened down again, she will take a proper holiday. Her last one was in July of 2005 – and was cut short by a series of suicide bombings on London tubes and buses. Along with every other senior member of staff she needed to be at her desk and on high alert immediately. This was emphasised by the fact that she was collected from her hotel in Senegal by a military helicopter. It landed on the tennis courts in the middle of the afternoon, to the bemusement and bewilderment of her partner at the time, who had, up till then, thought she did 'something in publishing'.

She has logged off and is stretched on the settee having a power nap when Carl comes into the kitchen. She opens her eyes and looks at her watch, it is nearly time to move – she assumes Carl has come to let her know he is getting ready to set off. Then she sees the expression on Carl's face, features set, eyes wide, lips tight. She knows that face, it is Carl at his most alert. As he comes closer she sees a cut in his left eyebrow, small but seeping blood which trickles unhindered down the side of his face. He crouches beside her, she is now sitting up and fully awake.

He whispers, "Sorry, Ma'am, we've got a small problem."

"Details?"

"We've had a visitor, I'm pretty sure he was flying solo, but when he doesn't check in more will come."

"How long?"

"I reckon we've got a couple of hours max before anybody else shows up, we need to be gone by then."

"Our visitor?"

"He's in the shed, he's not going anywhere for now. I intercepted him coming through the hedge by the west field. Here's his sidearm and his phone."

Alice takes them, she takes the magazine clip out, checks the gun is empty then puts them both deep inside her laptop bag. She doesn't expect the tech guys will get anything useful from either of them, but you never know.

"Okay, stick to the plan, I don't want anything to spook our guests. I'll have them ready to go in thirty minutes."

Carl nods, "I'll wait until you've gone then let a team know where they can come and collect the visitor – if his friends don't get here first."

He disappears back out of the door without waiting for a response. Alice waits for a moment, then follows him through the door and goes to the shed, she has something she wants to do before she wakes the others.

Opening the shed door, with its peeling paint and rusty latch, she holds up the torch that she picked up from the window ledge in the kitchen and points it into the darkness. There, sitting on the bare floor in the pool of light she has created, is a sorry looking man in black combat fatigues. His hands are zip tied behind his back and his ankles are similarly secured and joined to the large mower that is beside the back wall. On his forehead is a large angry-looking bump, there is blood in the corner of his mouth and one of his front teeth is missing.

"Name?"

"No comment." Unsurprisingly, he has an American accent.

"Service?"

"No comment."

She had expected nothing else and wasn't going to waste the short time they had trying to get anything from him, although she was sure Carl could persuade him to give up something if she asked him. No point now, they didn't have time.

"Well, Mr No Comment, I'm leaving shortly. Someone will come and pick you up later, if your own rag tag team don't rescue you first. Just so you know," her tone changes slightly as some of her anger comes to the fore, "I don't like armed men coming to my house in the middle of the night. If I see you again you will regret it, and if your boys arrive before I leave I'm coming back out here and I'll fucking shoot you. With your own gun. Understood?"

The man said nothing, but Alice had the pleasure of seeing him avert his eyes as a fleeting look of concern crossed his face. She smiles as she turns away and closes the door leaving him in darkness.

CHAPTER 12
Café

The morning brings heavy drizzle and bleary eyes. Alice is the only one of us who seems fully awake as she knocks on our doors and tells us it's time to get going now, it's still dark outside. Carl and the Audi, are nowhere to be seen, presumably he has already left. We forage for breakfast from what is available, Syd opts for the remains of the takeaway, Grace and Alice stick with coffee and I discover some energy bars – I need them - that I wash down with tea.

We leave the house as it is. Alice hurries us along, assuring us she has people coming who will clean up once we have left. We take our places in the Volvo and are soon on our way, with Alice keeping up a narrative about what she is doing and where we are going.

"I've got the place on the map, it looks straightforward. I hope Carl didn't wake you, did you sleep well? This road is bumpy, are you alright in the back?"

I decide she must have taken something in lieu of sleeping. Syd is occupying the front passenger seat again, she presses a button and the radio interrupts Alice's stream of consciousness before we can answer any of her questions – if that's what they were. The newsreader was talking about the rising rate of unemployment, before passing over to the weather report, then to Scott Mills excitedly playing a song by Bruno Mars, followed by One Direction. I quietly wish for it to be replaced by Mark Goodier or Janice Long, playing some of their weird and wonderful sessions with Nirvana or

Jesus Jones. Apparently, I am in the minority here though, so I quietly tolerate the music and try to block it out.

When Coventry arrives it is not what I expected. For some reason, probably my parochial localism, I had prepared myself for a grim, grey, industrial wasteland. Instead, I am greeted by a city like most others I have ever visited; suburbs, corner shops, larger supermarkets and car showrooms appear as we approach. The dark spires of the original heart of the city nest amongst the gleaming white and silver modernity of the newer buildings as we reach the centre.

Alice is following directions from a satnav that she must have programmed before we set off. She drives us through the early morning traffic lights, past roadworks, bus stops, cyclists and pedestrians until the small box on the dashboard announces that we are arriving at our destination in a stilted monotone voice. I look out at a waking street, old wooden shop fronts and red bricks – incongruous amongst the concrete and brushed metal maze we had driven through moments before. The Bean Counter is set between an estate agent's and a florist's, its window frame is painted a vibrant red, with a matching awning. A stream of red-painted tables and chairs are being arranged on the pavement, surrounding the shop door.

A man in his thirties with red trousers and a preposterous moustache appears to be coordinating things while two teenage girls, both with pony tails, bustle around setting up tables, making drinks for early birds and stocking the glass shelves on the counter.

Alice has pulled into a parking space a short distance from the café. She stops the car and looks up and down the street, taking in everything, before turning to Syd and telling her what she wants her to do.

Syd

As she walked through the door she furtively glanced around at the few customers already in the small room. Rick wasn't one of them. She let out a small sigh of relief, she wanted to be right about this – but she really didn't want to see him. She ordered a coffee from one of the pony tail girls and sat at one of the unoccupied tables as Alice had told her to. The coffee was indeed good, though maybe not quite living up to the hyperbole that had been used to describe it to her. She took her time, sipping slowly and watching customers come and go while the man with the moustache busily made drinks behind the counter.

Time passed slowly, men in suits hurried in and out, impatient to get to work, the tables started to fill and the steady stream of customers paid no notice of her. None of them were Rick. She was beginning to wonder if she should order another drink, unsure if it would be wise – or even possible – to drink coffee continuously all day, when Alice walked in.

She did not look in Syd's direction at all, she went to the counter and placed an order. Syd still wasn't sure she trusted her, why should she? Still, it wasn't as if she had any better options right now. Alice turned back from the counter, thanking the barista pleasantly. She walked past Syd without acknowledging her, carrying her coffee. Syd watched her pass, it was only as Alice left the café that she looked down and noticed a piece of paper folded on the table in front of her. She had no idea how Alice had put it there without her noticing, she picked it up and read it. 'Come back to the car.' printed in neat blue handwriting. Syd took her cue and went back into the street and to the car.

The passenger door opened for her as she arrived, she noticed that the back seat was empty now as she climbed in beside Alice.

"Where's mum?"

"Gone to get some rest."

Alice was holding a small screen on her lap. Syd recognised it as an iPad, although this was the first time she had seen one first hand. On the screen was a view of an interior, it took Syd a moment to realise it was the Bean Counter, looking towards the door from the slightly low perspective of the counter.

"Did you just…?"

"Yes, now we can watch who comes through the door from here, it'll save you having a caffeine overdose."

"Do you think this is a waste of time?"

"Not at all, even the smallest possibilities need to be followed up. You've given us some hope again, we'll fix this you know?"

"But what if he doesn't turn up?"

"Then he doesn't turn up. We'll regroup and rethink. Right now it's our best lead, and it's all thanks to you."

"But what if….?"

"Hey, no more 'what ifs', all you need to do for now is keep an eye on that screen and let me know if you see Rick. You're doing fantastically, don't overthink this."

"So we just sit and wait? All day?"

"All week if that's what it takes. Sorry, it's not always like the movies."

"You can say that again."

Alice smiled and they both looked down at the screen as a woman in a floral dress came through the door. Syd sighed audibly.

CHAPTER 13
Another House

Once Syd has gone into the Bean Counter Alice makes several phone calls. Grace and I sit in the back waiting to see what will happen next, both lost in our own silent reveries. I am wondering what, exactly, we are supposed to do now. I am also wondering if sharing the bed with Grace had meant anything, if I stood a chance, if that was what I wanted. One of my many questions is answered about ten minutes after Syd went in, unfortunately not the one I most wanted the answer to.

A motorbike growls noisily up the street and stops alongside the car, Alice opens the window and the anonymous motorcyclist passes her a parcel from inside his leather jacket before roaring off up the road. Following this, and before Alice has time to open the package, a red minicab pulls up with two wheels on the pavement across the street from where we are parked.

"I've called in some favours," Alice had turned to speak to us, "there's no need for all of us to sit here all day. That car will take you to a safe place where you can try and get some rest and wait for us."

"But what about Syd?" Grace asked.

"She's with me, she's safe. The best thing you can do is make sure you're refreshed and ready if anything does happen."

Grace is still reluctant to go.

"Come on," I say to her, "we're not being any help here are we?"

Reluctantly she gets out of the car and we transfer into the minicab. Alice passes me a handful of cash, neatly folded, as I get out.

"Don't use your cards, get anything you need."

The taxi ride is short, taking us via a series of confident shortcuts to an unassuming terraced house a short distance from the city centre.

"There you go mate, number 27," the driver informs us, before driving off, with a generous tip – fuck it, it's not my money!

Number 27 has a blue painted front door with an ornate brass doorknocker in the shape of a woodpecker. Before I can reach to tap its beak against the door, it is opened by a tall bearded man in workout clothes, he holds out a bunch of keys in one hand and picks up a small holdall with the other.

"I think it's all fairly tidy, sorry, but it was short notice. There's bread and milk in the kitchen, help yourself to anything you can find and make yourselves at home."

"Thanks," I reply as the man manoeuvres himself around Grace and me, into the street. He walks briskly up the road without glancing back. I look at Grace as we stand in front of the open door.

"I feel like I should carry you over the threshold or something."

"Pillock." She shoves me gently on the shoulder and follows me in.

We explore and inspect the house of the unnamed man. It is clearly his bachelor pad, no sign of kids or a partner. It is lived-in, but tidy, as he said. There are two bedrooms and a fold out settee that has been made up. On the kitchen counter is a carrier bag with a selection of new clothing: socks, underwear, tee shirts - all in a range of sizes to ensure we all have something clean to wear. There is also a bag of toiletries. I wonder how often he does this, who even knew that this sort of thing went on?

I busy myself finding the necessary ingredients to make two mugs of tea while Grace continues to investigate the house. She reappears as I am putting the mugs on the table.

"What now?" I ask.

"Well, I don't know about you, I'm going to have a shower. I feel like I could scrape the dirt off me, I must stink."

"I didn't like to mention it."

"Shut up, I'm going to throw my clothes down in a minute, will you put them in the washing machine please?"

"Yeah, I'll put mine in as well."

Grace takes her tea upstairs. Shortly afterwards there is the sound of running water and a soft whump as a bundle of clothes lands at the foot of the stairs, I collect them and catch a glimpse of her naked leg crossing the landing and disappearing into the bathroom. I cradle the bundle of clothes in my arms and can smell her on them. Not the stink she alluded to, but a familiar, comforting smell.

I add my own, less fragrant, clothes to the pile and figure out how to operate the washing machine - which switches to press and dials to turn, then sit in my boxers and tee shirt with a fresh cup of tea . Grace soon joins me; a towel is wrapped around her hair and she is swamped inside an enormous dressing gown.

"Better?"

"Much, thanks for the tea." She has swapped her empty mug for the fresh one I put on the table, she sips from it and smiles.

"Well, nothing's happening, I'm going to have a shower then a lay down, I'm knackered."

"I was thinking the same thing."

I follow Grace, catching glimpses of her feet as she climbs the stairs. I feel like a Victorian voyeur watching her well-turned ankles as she ascends. In spite of knowing how ridiculous it is, I found myself feeling aroused. I veer off to the bathroom and scrub away the dirt and sweat in the shower. The clean new boxers and tee shirt feel good against my skin as I join Grace in the bedroom, laying down next to her. I wonder what would happen if I were to kiss her, but when I look across I see she has already closed her eyes and is breathing slowly. I surrender to the inevitable and slide into sleep.

The sound of the front door wakes me with a start, momentarily disorientated as I try to remember where I am, followed by panic about who might be at the door.

"Mum?"

It's Syd's voice, I feel a little foolish for thinking it could be anybody else.

Footsteps approach on the stairs and the door is pushed open as I am sitting up. Grace is also awake now, she sits up quickly, causing the oversized dressing gown to slide off her shoulder as she does so. This reveals most of her breast that she quickly covers again, but both Syd and I saw it. A big step up from ankles and feet in my opinion.

"You two, what are you like?" It is a teasing admonition, given with a cheeky smile.

Grace protests, "It's not like that."

But it's too late, the door is already closing.

"I'll see you downstairs, when you're done and decent," Syd's disembodied voice calls.

We look at one another and laugh.

"I wish I'd done something to earn that telling off," says Grace.

"Do you?"

I think I see a flicker of a smile in the corner of Grace's mouth, I definitely see a roll of her eyes as she commands me to go and collect her clothes from the dryer. I do as I am told, trotting past Alice and Syd who are making tea and rummaging in the fridge. I acknowledge them as I pass with my arms full of clothes; warm, scented with lavender and hopelessly intertwined. In the back of my mind a small voice is nagging, whispering – 'what if?'

What if I had been braver when we were young?

What if I had made more of an effort?

What if I hadn't let go of the one good thing I had had?

What if I hadn't been such a dick?

For years now Grace has been 'off limits'. When my thoughts had strayed to her it had never been with any hope or expectations, she was married with a kid. But now, well now things are different. But right now definitely doesn't feel like the right time.

I pass Grace her clothes and take my own into the bathroom. We arrive in the kitchen within moments of each other and sit at the table. Syd looks at us with raised eyebrows as she pours tea from the large brown pot and Alice moves things out of the fridge to start cooking. She turns and joins us as her mug is filled.

"Whose house is this?" asks Syd.

"A friend who owes me a favour."

"I'm guessing you had no luck at the coffee shop," I say.

"No, it was always a long shot, but it's still our best bet at the moment. Carl's in Liverpool, he drew a blank too, we'll start again tomorrow."

The evening ticks away, we eat, plan for tomorrow and manage to agree on something we all find acceptable on the TV – a detective show filmed on a Caribbean island somewhere. The beaches and blue skies are inviting, gruesome murders notwithstanding - although none of us really watches, as we discuss events, prepare for tomorrow and find things that have to be done. Eventually Syd's yawns prompt us to accept defeat and draw the day to a close. Alice had long since retreated to the kitchen to do whatever it is she does on her laptop and phone. She never seems to stop. Syd disdainfully examines the clean underwear that has been left for her, then goes to shower. Grace and I return to the bedroom and adopt the same 'just friends' sleeping position that we had been in earlier.

Alice

Having managed to sleep for a short while on the sofa bed, Alice was up with the sun. She woke Syd in plenty of time for her to dress and eat before going back to the coffee shop, to be there when it opened. She hadn't factored in the length of time that Syd would spend getting ready, but had left enough margin for error that it didn't matter too much. They were parked back in the same street as yesterday, before any of the shops had opened. The Bean Counter's blinds were still pulled halfway down, exactly as they had been when they finally left yesterday afternoon.

Alice wasn't convinced that anything would come of this, but it felt good to be doing something proactive, out from behind her desk and doing some field work again. All the more so because, even though she was nowhere near retirement age, she was planning to hand over the reins to someone else next year and start to live a less hectic life. She still didn't know what that would look like for her, probably not tending the roses outside a rural cottage or cruising the Bahamas. She had tentatively planned to move into her grandparents farmhouse, the recent visit had only reminded her how much she enjoyed being there, but definitely finding time to travel without working, write and enjoy some of the finer, more leisurely pursuits that had been eluding her. So it was most likely that this would be her last outing, if that was the case she wanted to make it count for something.

The small screen on her lap once again showed the view from the shop counter, looking down through the dimly lit tables and chairs directly at the door. As they watched the door opened, and from the street Alice could see moustache man with his jangling bunch of keys entering the building. Shortly afterwards a delivery van parked across the front of the building and the days supplies of fresh milk and baked goods were carried inside. Moustache man locked the door again and all went quiet.

Now the street around them was starting to wake up and come to life, people arrived, shutters came up, sign boards were placed on the pavement and cards in windows were flipped over to read 'open'. The Bean Counter also started to emerge from its slumber; the pony tail girls arrived and set out the bright red tables and chairs on the pavement as a smattering of customers in business suits and office frocks began to enter, then exited with coffee in takeaway cups. Alice settled down.

Thirty minutes later she was about to ask Syd if she would like a coffee, a chance to stretch her legs and something to drink would be a good thing. As she turned to ask her Syd spoke, "There he is, bastard!"

The last word was spat out with venom and Alice immediately looked back down at the screen with the feed from the shop. It only showed one of the pony tail girls clearing a table. She looked over to Syd and saw that her gaze was focussed not on the café, but on a figure approaching from the end of the street. He was barely recognisable from the fuzzy CCTV images that Alice had seen, but Syd was clearly in no doubt – why wouldn't she be? Syd reached down to the door handle and Alice gently put her hand on her shoulder, "Not now. Stay low and wait."

Syd looked disappointed, but did as she was asked, sliding herself down into the seat and glaring daggers at Rick while muttering obscenities under her breath as he passed them and went into the café.

"Aren't you going to get him?"

"Yes, but not right now," Alice replied as she rapidly typed something on her phone. She didn't blame Syd for wanting to confront him, but now was not the time. She would get her chance later, if all went to plan. "You stay here and lay low, okay?"

"I suppose."

Alice ignored the daggers now being redirected at her and watched both the small monitor and the door of the Bean Counter, her fingers dashing over her phone as she texted once more. As Rick came out, with a coffee cup and a small bag in hand she stepped out of the car and started to walk along the pavement, keeping pace with him on the other side of the road. Her phone was held to her ear and she had a look of practised nonchalance.

It had been a while since she had needed to follow anyone. She automatically fell back into the routines and techniques that had been drilled into her many years before, feeling a small buzz of excitement at being back in the field, doing the sort of surveillance and covert work she had enjoyed when she was younger. Usually she left this sort of activity to other people nowadays, but needs must. She knew that a middle-aged woman was as anonymous as anybody else, if not more so. Casually looking down at her phone as she kept pace with the man across the street, she started to cross the road before they reached the junction that Rick had appeared from minutes before. Her pace slowed, maintaining a distance between them, then became brisker as he disappeared around the corner.

Sometimes things just work out. He only went a short distance further, then stopped by a door sandwiched between the front of a pizza shop and a shop window filled with mannequins draped in exquisitely colourful saris. He fumbled his keys out and opened the door. As she paused to look at the brightly draped material and clothes the faded red door was closing again, she looked and saw that it was the entrance to two flats. One doorbell had the name Sophie next to it on a sticky label, the other was blank. She continued to walk in the same direction she had been travelling, taking a longer route that took her around the block, eventually arriving back at the car. As she got there she leant in, put her phone down and smiled at Syd.

"Didn't you get him?" she asked.

"He's enjoying his coffee and muffin, I hope he makes the most of it, he's going to get a surprise soon. We're going to stay here and make sure he doesn't go anywhere. Once the back-up team turn up then we'll have things to do and places to go, have your seatbelt on ready."

Alice then strolled back to the corner of the street and chose a convenient and discrete bench that offered a good clear view of the flat door. In a little over 10 minutes a black van arrived, identical to one that Syd would have recognised. It parked on the road near to the flat, and waited for Alice's instructions to be relayed to them.

Alice returned to where Syd was waiting, got in and pulled out of the parking space, slowly working her way back through the traffic to the house.

Rick

Kicking the front door closed behind him with his foot he went up the dimly lit staircase. Balancing his muffin on top of his coffee cup, he selected the key he needed, inserted it into the lock and let himself into the flat.

Inside was tidy almost to the point of being spartan: uncluttered surfaces, minimal belongings on display, no ornaments or photos. The main feature of the kitchen area was an ostentatiously large, polished black and chrome coffee machine. Everything else in the living area spoke of impermanence.

It had been like this since he came back from travelling around the edges of Europe after he finished his computer science degree. In the last few weeks of his trip he had ended up in a small coastal town in Albania. The lively bustle and predictably hot weather had drawn him to the beaches in the south, where he had been looking for some work to subsidise the meagre amount of cash he still had left.

With a promise of food in exchange for 'doing a few small jobs', he had been cleaning the outside furniture at a café. It was hot, sweaty work and the café owner had been meticulously checking the quality of his exertions at regular, irritating, intervals.

In ones and twos a group of men had congregated at the tables, shouting greetings and ordering drinks as each new arrival appeared. They had bustled and fussed around noisily, then, unexpectedly, one of the men invited him to stop clearing up cigarette buts from the patio and surrounding plant pots, and join them to eat. The opportunity to eat without having to complete his labours was not to be turned down, he took them up on their offer and ended up spending the evening in their company, to the evident annoyance of the café proprietor.

The time passed pleasantly, eating, drinking and joining in the conversation where he could. The men, who were not European but Egyptian, all spoke good English and took it in turns conversing with him, while the others spoke in their native Arabic. At the end of the night one of the men, the one who had asked him to join them, asked where he was staying.

"I was going to sleep on the beach, I'm nearly broke. I'll have to go back to the UK soon."

"No," the man insisted, "not the beach, you will be my guest tonight."

There was no arguing, and given the opportunity not to spend another night in al fresco discomfort, Rick returned to the man's home and slept in a bed for the first time in several days. He slept well and ate a hearty breakfast the next morning. When he suggested he would be on his way soon, his host appeared indignantly offended.

"What will people think if I don't show you my hospitality? You must stay another night."

The night turned into two, then three. Each evening various people would arrive at the house, meeting with his host, Abasi. They insisted he sat with them, sharing stories and coffee – really good coffee - late into the night, making him feel like part of a family. Little by little he came to think of them as friends, and by equally small increments he came to know what it was they met to discuss and organise. They wanted to find a way to usurp the government in their homeland and reclaim their families birthrights.

His own family relationships had been strained even before his mother died, his dad's new partner had not been an adequate replacement in his eyes and they had all grown apart over the last few years. This had been not least because of his left-leaning political views, which had managed to further estrange both his deeply conservative father and his older brother.

The visitors to the house wanted change, not a violent revolution, but a modern one, using unconventional and underhand techniques to make a difference. They were earnest and passionate about what they wanted to do, but not practical. With his background in computing he was able to suggest things that might work more effectively than the ideas they had proposed, contributing to their hypothetical and nebulous plans. He quickly became known as 'the computer guy' and his presence at their informal and noisy meetings became less as an observer and more as an advisor. Then, early one morning Abasi woke him, "Get dressed, we're going for a drive."

He was driven to a small cluster of wind-blown buildings in the scorched mountains of a sparsely populated area of the desert, where his real education began.

*

Taking the lid off his coffee he sipped it carefully as he sat down at the kitchen table. A small smile curled up from the edge of his mouth as he took a second sip and powered up his laptop. He opened his emails and started to read, the smile growing as he proceeded.

It seemed as though his last job had been successful, managing to spread distrust and paranoia over a broad area. He had kind of liked the girl, but there was always going to be collateral damage, he had known that from the outset. Now he was going to enjoy some down time before his next instructions came through. He hoped it would be another university, they were fun. Realistically it was more likely he was going to be sent to another of those disgusting 'peace camps' with a bunch of old hippies again, most likely at Hinkley power station in Somerset, where protests were already underway.

Wherever it was, his brief would be the same as it had been for the last two years: arrive, infiltrate the group as best he could (usually by isolating someone that he could work with) then do his thing – making it look as if the group was working against the state, or any state in fact. Then, once the twin seeds of distrust and discord had been sown, leave them to it. All of these capitalist governments were the same, so busy bickering amongst themselves that they could never make a definite decision about anything, it was too easy sometimes, playing them off against one another.

This kind of subversion had been much harder for his predecessors, but with the advent of computer technology new opportunities were now available, if you were good enough to take advantage of them. And he was good, he knew it. The layers of protection he had wrapped around himself were thick, even if he said so himself – masterful. The chances of anything leading back to him were zero.

Once he had passed his hard drive over to Abasi – who would pass it to someone else who would add yet more layers of mischief to his work – this job would be complete. Until then he was planning on taking some well-earned time off. Nothing elaborate, he would probably spend a lot of it reading, researching what he thought would be his next placement and drinking some damn fine coffee.

He sat back and looked over at his muffin on the kitchen counter. 'Later', he thought, 'there's plenty of time.' Then he leaned back and enjoyed his coffee.

He was deciding what he should reheat for his tea when the front door burst open. He was still crouching by the freezer, one hand on the open door, when a pair of black clad legs appeared in front of him. He looked up at the hulking figure standing with his hands on his hips and an unpleasant grin on his face.

"Rick I presume?"

The flat was rapidly filling up with other men and women in unmarked uniforms with weapons in their hands. He knew the game was up, but still looked round, hoping against hope that there would be a point of egress, a way to escape - or at least a chance to destroy the laptop. There was none, the incursion had been so swift and efficient that there was nothing he could do.

"Up you get then, you're coming for a ride. Unless you feel like telling me where the drive is first."

His heart was racing, he said nothing.

"Maybe I could have a quick go at beating it out of you – you little shit."

Now he was scared. He had always known that there was a chance he would be caught, although he had been so full of his own brilliance he had never truly believed it would happen. Now, confronted with a large, armed man he understood what hubris was. He started to reach for his phone.

The man standing in front of him didn't move to stop him, he just shook his head slowly and held his hand out. Rick reluctantly passed his phone to the man, who slid it into a pocket then motioned for him to stand up and pointed to the door where two burly figures waited for him.

CHAPTER 14
Wait

I am woken by the sounds of Syd and Alice leaving. It's still early. I slide quietly out of the bed, not wanting to disturb Grace, and go to the kitchen after I hear the front door click closed. With a mug of hot tea in front of me I sit quietly and run through the sequence of events that have led me to here. Memories from 25 years ago overlap with the present, and I try to make sense of how I am feeling. The same dread and foreboding from my teenage years have resurfaced, memories of those difficult days – and of Lisa – still hang around the edges of my thoughts. I wonder if it is fate that is pushing me and Grace back towards one another, and if she is feeling the same pull of attraction that I am. I have tried to tell myself that it is just the circumstances we are in, that Grace has moved on and it is just wishful thinking. I don't know if she is feeling anything towards me, as previously noted I am not good at reading signals.

My thoughts are interrupted by the sound of footsteps on the stairs. I am already putting the kettle on to boil again when Grace comes in wrapped in the oversized dressing gown she found yesterday.

"Morning."

"Morning, did they already leave?" She yawns as she finished speaking and I watched her as she runs her hands through her bed-tousled hair.

"Yeah, about half an hour ago, I'm surprised they didn't wake you."

"I guess I was tired, it's been a busy couple of days."

"You don't say? You know I can go out if you want some time to yourself, a bit of peace and quiet. I've been kind of foisted on you. I feel like a spare wheel."

"Are you kidding? Catching up with you is about the only good thing that's come out of this so far. I don't know why I didn't get in touch sooner."

"Because you had other things to think about?"

"True, but it's good having you here. It helps me forget how much of a dick Ed is – was."

"What, and I'm not?"

"Not so much."

"I was though, I should've been there for you."

She kind of shrugs and smiles as she crosses the kitchen and pulls me towards her to kiss my cheek. At least I thought that was what it was, but at the last minute she shimmies and twists so the kiss lands on my mouth, and stays there for longer than a 'friend kiss'. She pushes her body against mine as she kisses me, I guess that answers the question I had been asking myself earlier. I am painfully aware of the fact that I am only wearing a tee shirt and boxer shorts now, they are doing little to nothing to hide my reaction to her embrace. Grace smiles, a wicked smile that I remember well, then pushes harder against me, her kisses becoming more intense and urgent. Abruptly she stops and steps away, turning towards the stairs, "Come on then, don't keep a lady waiting."

I'm not sure if what I am feeling is excitement, relief or nervousness – it's probably a mixture of all three. I follow Grace up the stairs to the bedroom, she turns and holds me. Beneath her sensualness and urgency I feel her nervousness too. I'm about to ask if she's sure when she shrugs the dressing gown off and lets it drop to the floor, revealing her naked body. Not the time for questions or conversation now then, time for rediscovering something I had thought I'd lost.

*

Later, lying in the bed, satisfied and sweaty, my mind is once again in turmoil. Is this just a one-off? Is it the rekindling of our youthful relationship? Whatever it is, it was good, just what the doctor ordered. I start to speak, "When this is over…"

"Not now, we don't need to decide anything right now, just enjoy the moment."

"I am, I did. But I messed up before didn't I?"

"No, it just wasn't right. I understand why now, I'm sorry I didn't get it at the time."

"It was never your fault, you don't need to apologise. I was pretty stupid back then – I'm not much better now, but I'm trying."

"I'd say you turned out pretty good, all things considered. Alice seems to trust you, and Syd told me she thinks you're cool."

I pause and run this through my mind. In spite of what she had told me I had never really believed that Alice would have any opinion about me at all, apart from possibly contempt - driven by her knowledge of the true depths of my teenage stupidity. As for Syd, working with kids I know that 'cool' is high praise indeed- although I'm not sure what I did to merit it. Grace breaks into my thoughts, "I kept all the letters you sent me you know, much to Ed's disgust."

"I would pretend to be surprised, but I've got yours too." It is a sizeable bundle of well-thumbed, multi-hued envelopes that get called out of retirement from their box in the bottom of the wardrobe when I am feeling maudlin. "I think I've read them enough times to have them memorised now. We were good, weren't we?"

"Maybe we still are."

We kiss and I run my hands down Grace's back, enjoying the feel of her smooth skin and the way she responds to my touch. Before we can get more involved, the sound of the front door breaks the moment. We pull apart and then both start looking for clothes and rapidly dressing, just like the time we nearly got caught out by Grace's returning parents one summer morning. We hurry down the stairs in the bare minimum of clothes to give an air of decency. Our arrival is greeted by an eye roll from Syd and a wink in my direction from Alice – what is it with the winking?

"You need to finish dressing and get ready to go," she tells us.

"Why? What's happened? Where are we going?" asks Grace.

"I'll explain on the way."

"Did you find him?"

"Yes, let's get this show on the road, shall we?"

"Are you okay Syd?"

"I'm fine, go and get dressed, lovebirds."

"It's not like it seems."

"It probably is, it's okay mum, I'm pleased for you both. Now get dressed."

I take no part whatsoever in the exchange, feeling even more like a guilty teenager. We go upstairs and finish dressing before collecting the minimal belongings we have managed to retain over the last few days, which amounts to very little for me and only marginally more for Grace. The earlier relaxed mood has changed dramatically now, Grace hurries to get back to Syd. I am only moments behind her but they are already standing by the open door waiting for me, Alice is in the car outside with the engine running. I look guiltily around the mess we have left in the kitchen before getting into the car which starts to pull away even before I have buckled my seatbelt.

"The bastard came to the coffee shop, we found him."

"Where is he now?" I ask.

Alice answers, "He's being collected."

I know, from personal experience, what this means. So does Syd too I guess. I do not feel sorry for him. I also think I know where we will be going to next, and I'd really rather not. I am thinking about this and miss part of a conversation, I tune back in to hear Grace asking, "What will happen to him then?"

"Nothing's been decided yet," answers Alice. "It depends on what he has to say for himself."

There is a collective, pensive silence at this. I settle back uneasily, looking out of the window and preparing myself for the long journey ahead. I am surprised when we pass a sign for the M6 and Alice does not take the turning. My curiosity does not remain piqued for long though, the car turns into a gateway with a sign proudly proclaiming the site to be the home of Coventry Welsh Rugby Football Club. As we come to a halt, I see a helicopter in the middle of the pitch, with two men in black jumpsuits standing beneath its slowly rotating blades. A pair of curious onlookers stand outside the clubhouse, with brooms and dusting cloths in their hands. Alice is first out of the car, we follow her across the patches of mud and miserable clumps of grass towards the waiting helicopter.

I feel a tremble of anticipation, I've never been in a helicopter before. This does not seem an appropriate time to announce how excited I am, Syd however has no such qualms, "Are we going in that?" The childlike rising pitch of her voice is clearly audible over the sound of the engines as they start up. Alice does not dignify the question with an answer, she just smiles at Syd and nods, then turns to speak to one of the men standing at the ready. The man she has spoken to climbs into the cockpit while the second man walks off towards the abandoned car. Alice ushers us into the back of the helicopter and directs us towards lap straps and ear defenders as the tempo of the rotors above us gradually increases in intensity. She gives the pilot a thumbs up as the final strap is cinched into place and we lurch abruptly into the sky, the rugby club rapidly shrinking and disappearing as we tilt forward and start our journey.

Grace reaches over and grips my hand as the world races by beneath us and a crackly version of Alice's voice appears inside my headset, "Everyone okay?"

I give her a thumbs up, I know I am grinning like a kid in a sweetshop -that is giving away free puppies - on a cancelled school day. I can't help myself. I watch out of the window as the landscape scrolls by beneath us. We hardly seem to be moving, in spite of the speed that we must be travelling. It occurs to me that I did not have time to pee in the rush to leave the house, I'll just have to hold it in and hope that we are not airborne for too long.

As I get gradually more uncomfortable, Grace starts to relax and slowly releases her grip on my hand. She leans across to share my window, pointing at landmarks and features as they pass beneath us. I relish her closeness, but am not so keen on the way she is leaning on my bladder. Our ears are filled with Syd's enthusiastic commentary on the progress of the flight.

The landscape changes, it gradually runs out of houses and buildings, until all that is left is an ocean of green and purple. A black scar guides us toward a rectangular enclosure and a single grey building in the shape of an upper case H. It increases in size as we angle our descent towards it. My guess about where we are going is confirmed, which adds another layer to my feeling of discomfort. This time it is me that grips Grace's hand as we swoop over the fence and settle onto an area of grass within the enclosure.

The first thing I do when I disembark, after ducking under the still revolving blades, is to walk briskly to the edge of the grass and relieve myself against a fence post. It is not a moment too soon, I don't care about what the others think, they are pretending to ignore me anyway. Next I fish in my pocket for the crumpled packet with its two remaining cigarettes. I light one, cupping the lighter from the draft created by the helicopter rotors, as I re-join the group. I duck involuntarily as the helicopter rises noisily back into the air behind me, dust and debris fly around me as it clatters off to its next destination.

"What now?" I ask Alice over the receding noise.

"Now we wait for Rick to join us. It may be a while, so I suggest we all get comfortable. Mrs Baker will see to some refreshments and I'll join you in a bit, I have some things to sort out."

Mrs Baker was standing, smiling, by the doors, where she is waiting for us to follow her inside. I take my time, finishing my cigarette before following the others back into the windowless building.

Alice

Back in her office Alice took a deep breath, exhaled, then looked at the messages on her phone as she poured some freshly brewed coffee. She allowed herself a smile as she reflected on how the day was going, while it was true that not much had gone to plan so far, it was working out now. It had always been her habit to have a backup plan and a backup, backup plan, setting up failsafe options, fallback opportunities and contingency strategies. When she was younger her old boss, O'Brien, had gently teased her about this. He had also made it clear that he thoroughly approved and encouraged her to keep doing it.

He once told her that her dad, an old colleague of his, had been the same; "He always thought of the 'what ifs?', he treated everything like a large-scale, real-life chess game." This made sense to Alice, her dad had taught her to play at an early age, six or seven years-old. They played as often as they could when he was at home, with Alice having some successes over the years. It was only many years later that she realised he had been pulling his punches.

As she got older and busier it had been 'their thing'. He had a board set up in his tiny office room, when they got an opportunity they would sit quietly across from one another and absorb themselves in battle – only ever face to face, he assured her it was a social game. Before he died, after a short and painful illness, she would win maybe one game in three, although by then she had started to pull some punches of her own. The companionable silence as they faced each other across the 64 squares, punctuated by occasional understated conversations, were some of her happiest memories of her dad. The rare times that he relaxed, smiling approvingly when she boxed him in, furrowing his brow in mock concentration while he plotted his next move. Then doing his awful impression of Frank Spencer that he knew would make her laugh however much she tried not to.

She sensed that the real-life game she was involved in now was reaching a critical point. Whatever happened next would need the right counter-move from her if she was going to help Syd. No O'Brien or dad to defer to now, just her own best judgement and instincts.

Sipping her coffee she sat at her computer and checked her updates while simultaneously calling Carl to give him last-minute instructions and get a progress reports.

He is close to arriving at the address she has given him, the pick-up team is already watching the flat, waiting nearby for him to get there. He is planning to acquire the target within the next thirty minutes. He has their best search team ready to go in once the property is empty. Alice has already authorised the team to dig as deep as they need to, to leave no stone unturned, take the plaster off the wall if necessary. She tells Carl he is to stay at the flat until they are done, not to travel in with Rick – leave that to the escorts.

This done she called Mrs Baker on the intercom to give her a rough idea of the arrival time of their new guest, reminding her that nobody else should know that he is coming, she does not tell Mrs Baker that she suspects a leak. No problem there, Mrs Baker was always a 'need to know' type of person. She had already made sure everything was ready, just as Alice had known she would do.

Now her mind moved on to considering what would happen next for Syd. It had not been her intention for everyone to end up back here and she was mindful of how difficult it would be for them. After dealing with Rick, her main priority was moving them on. That, and finding out how her nocturnal visitor had found out where they were, but that was for another day.

Another gulp of coffee and a chance to take stock. An element of luck, certainly, but also a set of calm and level heads working together to keep ahead of the game. Taking her mug with her, she goes to the meeting room where the others are waiting for her.

They look disorientated and weary, not surprising after the last 48 hours. She reminds herself to check they have clean clothes, toiletries, and anything else they might need, although she is certain that Mrs Baker would already have this in hand – has probably done it already. It will be harder than providing clean underwear, if not impossible, to get that frightened, haunted look off their faces.

"Thank you for your patience. I'm sorry we've ended up back here, I know it's not where you wanted – or expected – to be right now," she says as she joins them at the table. She does not anticipate, or wait for, a response.

"Rick should be joining us later this afternoon, until then please make yourselves as comfortable as you can. Mrs B can provide most things, just ask. You are all free to move around the building for now, or to go outside. As soon as I have any more information for you I'll let you know, but for now just sit tight and try not to worry."

"What will happen when Rick gets here?" asks Syd.

"I'm not sure at the moment, I've got a lot of questions for him, and I know other people do too. It depends a lot on what he has to say for himself. I'm hopeful that things will be able to be resolved quickly now that we have him."

"Will Syd be able to come home then?" asks Grace.

"Soon, I hope. There are lots of things that need to happen first, until then please have a rest, have something to eat and try not to worry. If Mrs B has forgotten anything, which is unlikely, just find her and ask."

She felt like her responses had been politicians' answers; saying nothing while you appear to be saying something. Although she had experience of this in other areas of her work it does not sit well with her now. She wanted to give them more detailed answers, explain what the possibilities were and what variables there might be. When things start to happen, they will probably happen quickly, until then the deeply unglamourous side of her work – the waiting – is all that is on offer. She thanks them and takes her leave, going directly to the tech area where she finds Bob. She gives him the phone that Carl took from the previous night's visitor, "A burner, but see if you can get anything."

"I'll do what I can."

"Thanks Bob."

She then listens as he runs through what they have uncovered, overheard or found out on the internet grapevine that might help her when Rick arrives. It is precious little so far. During this conversation she gets the message that Rick is safely on his way.

"I'm going to have another phone for you to dig into soon, and hopefully a computer too, if we're lucky."

These will be delivered by a motorcycle courier as soon as Carl has retrieved them from the flat, she can see from his expression that Bob is looking forward to performing his magic, using the dark arts of the tech guys. She returns to her office and does the only thing she can do now – she waits.

CHAPTER 15
Stranger

There is only so much tea I can drink. I have wandered up and down the corridors twice. Most of the doors are locked with card readers, the ones that are open offer nothing to hold my interest: small meeting rooms, bedrooms, sparsely furnished offices. The only other person I see is Mrs B. Of course I saw her a few days ago, but it was brief. I hadn't realised from those passing encounters just how many wrinkles and creases she has. It is not an unkindly face, but it definitely has a look that says, 'I may not be in charge, but I run this place', much like the look that a seasoned school administrator can give to anyone who transgresses in their domain. She looks at me over the top of her glasses as I hover in her office doorway, catching me staring at her she asks if she can help. I fumble for a suitable excuse for being here in the first place.
"I was just looking for…" I falter.

"Something to distract yourself? I think you've tried all the doors on this level now," her face breaks into a smile, the wrinkles coalesce and for a moment she reminds me of my grandma. "I have to say, it's quite irregular having people running around the place like this. You have certainly grown into a fine young man. I can ask someone to bring up some books or games if you want."

Young man? It's a while since anybody called me that, and of course she remembers me. I bet she could write the history of this place – if it was allowed, which it probably isn't. Also, 'this level' and 'bring up', I had suspected that there was more to this place than met the eye, so a sub-level - maybe more than one. The stairwell must be behind one of the locked doors.

"That would be great, any chance of a radio?"

"I'm afraid not, they don't work here – too much interference."

It follows, I am not over surprised.

"Never mind, anything to do would be great, thanks."

"You're welcome, another small smile makes the wrinkles at the side of her eyes deepen briefly, "I'll ask Dan to get something, anything else?"

"No, we're good thanks."

And we are, food, in the form of snacks and sandwiches, and beverages had been arriving regularly, bought in on a small trolley by a man with short hair, greying at the temples and thin lips, who I guess is Dan. I am back in the meeting room where Grace and Syd are engrossed in conversation. I sink into my seat, deep in thought, wondering if my parents have missed me yet, wondering if anyone has missed me really – I'm not exactly what you'd call sociable. I am not tuned in to what Syd and Grace are talking about, it's just background to my inner monologue.

"Isn't that right?"

This is clearly directed at me, it shakes me from my ruminations and I look up to see Grace looking at me expectantly.

"Sorry, no idea, I was a million miles away."

"I was telling Syd how things that seem important now will change over time, in a few years her priorities will change."

"I suppose."

I look at the two of them, sitting close together. Syd looks so much like Grace did at her age, she looks so young. Were we really that young once? What happened to the years? And why did I waste them looking for something that I already had, but let go?

"Is that it? 'I suppose'. Thanks for your words of wisdom."

Syd laughs, it's good to see her laugh, and there hasn't been much to laugh about the last few days. I collect my thoughts and try again,

"Yeah, some things look big from the front and small from behind. Sometimes you think you've got it all sorted out, made all the right calls, done what needs to be done. But later, sometimes much, much later, you realise that you could have done things differently. You just have to accept it – or hope that maybe you'll get another chance."

I'm looking at Grace while I speak, she holds my gaze. Syd is so much more mature than I was when I was her age, maybe even more mature than I am now. She gets up.

"I'm going to see Mrs Baker, ask if she can find me some Haribo. I'll see you two later."

She leaves the room with a glance back over her shoulder.

"Pick your time," Grace says, with a flicker of a smile.

"What other time was there?"

She nods, then crosses the room and sits on the chair next to mine.

"Let's get through this first, then see what happens. You've never been far from my thoughts, although – for the record - you didn't make all those choices by yourself."

"I know, I've made plenty of bad choices of my own since then though. At least I don't have a green lizard tattoo."

Grace laughs at this, then leans across to kiss me. Just as our lips touch the door opens and Dan carries in an armful of board games, books, packs of cards and a selection of sweets – including the Haribo that Syd had requested.

"Here you go, let Mrs B know if you need anything else," he promptly turns back and leaves the room.

"We will, thanks a lot."

The door closes and I'm not even sure if he heard me, if he did I didn't catch a response. Then he's gone and we are alone again. We kiss, properly this time, and I feel the way I did on the beach at midnight, the first time we kissed. I am lost in the smell and feel of her when the door opens again, this time it bursts open and a whirlwind of Syd enters the room.

"He's here, they've got him. He's here. I was in the office talking to Mrs Baker when I heard it on her intercom."

So, things are starting to happen. Maybe now things can all be sorted out and normal life can resume; although I know deep down that my normal has been turned on its head. We go together to Mrs Baker's office, where she tells us in no uncertain terms to go back and wait, that a lot of things need to happen now and that someone will come and tell us as soon as there is something to tell.

We go disconsolately back to the meeting room and I start to sift through the selection that Dan has bought us. Syd comes in and picks up a bag of gummy sweets and a small rectangular box,

"Uno! I love Uno, who wants to play?"

In spite of the situation, it proves to be a good diversion. Syd has an elaborate scoring system which seems to be rigged against me, and Grace shows an unexpectedly competitive and ruthless streak that is closely matched by her daughter. We are deeply involved in a round, which I am losing again, when Dan arrives with a trolley loaded with a small buffet, he leaves it near the door and exits as promptly as he is able. I wonder if he has cooked it himself, or if he is just in charge of delivery. Whatever, the smell is delicious and we put the game on hold while we eat.

Replete, I stretch, "I'm going to use the loo before you two start beating me again, I can't lose on a full bladder."

I use the facilities then decide to step outside before I return. In the west the sun is ending its daily arch, kissing the horizon and bathing the landscape in a gold and orange glow that is taking the last of the day's warmth with it. I fish in my pocket for the last remaining cigarette; it is twisted inside the squashed packet. I straighten it out and locate the lighter. I am half way through it when Grace comes out.

"Here you are, we thought you'd got lost."

"Caught," I say holding the cigarette for her to see, "I really don't smoke any more, not until I got back here."

"This is really hard for you isn't it?"

"It's easier than it was last time, and easier with you here."

I crush the half-smoked cigarette under my foot and embrace her, holding her in my arms as she pushes against me.

"Do you think we can? When this is over, can we try again?" I ask.

"I don't know, there would need to be some changes."

"I know, I think I'm ready now."

"You need to be sure."

Of course I do, I can see in her eyes that she is scared of being hurt again, why wouldn't she be? Hurting her is the last thing I would want to do, but I know from past experience that I am capable of hurting people without even thinking about it. In fact, on reflection, not thinking about it may have been part of the problem.

"I'm sure."

We kiss. Behind her I see a bright glow approaching the gate in the gloom. I guess I must have stopped returning her kiss, Grace pulls away and follows my gaze to the road. From here I can see the car is black and moving at speed, a final ray of sunlight flashes on its silver grill. It flickers as if it is sending a morse code message, 'I'm coming, I'm coming.'

The car comes to an abrupt halt a hundred metres from the gatehouse and the driver's door opens. A figure steps out, silhouetted by the setting sun and wearing a full-length coat that flaps around him in the wispy moorland breeze. He walks to the front of the car and stands in front of the headlights that cast a corona around him, giving him an almost mythical appearance, like a gunslinger from an old western.

I become aware of a flurry of activity in the previously deserted area we are standing in. Dan has appeared and is approaching the gate, behind us others are coming through the door and following him. They are all carrying what look like serious-business firearms to me. Their previously laid-back personas have disappeared.

The diminutive figure of Mrs Baker appears by our sides, in her slacks and cardigan, the gentle smile from earlier now gone.

"It would probably be best if you go back inside," she says, indicating the door with a liver-spotted, knotted hand that is holding a pistol. This is clearly an instruction rather than a recommendation, Grace and I start to walk back as Alice, also carrying a gun, hurries past us.

"What's going on?" I ask.

"I don't know yet, go on inside and I'll come and see you as soon as I can."

Alice has a look of authority and determination as she strides towards the gate. I hear a thunk as the door closes behind us and locks shut.

Grace relates the sequence of events to Syd when we get back to the room. She is unable to elaborate any more than telling her that a car arrived and everyone came running out armed to the teeth. This adds a layer of nervousness and uncertainty about what is going on, another twist on what has already been a very winding road. Nobody feels like resuming our game, or reading, or talking. In Syd's words – "Wow! This shit just keeps getting weirder."

CHAPTER 16
Meeting

It is not a long wait to find out what's going on, but it is a wait we make in nervous silence. Mrs Baker comes into the room, unarmed now, she sits down and smooths the front of her trousers then clears her throat and addresses Syd.

"I don't usually get involved in this part of the business, but everyone else is busy right now and needs must, it seems to be that sort of a day. The boss is with a visitor, he has asked to speak with you. She has told him that she will ask you, which is why I'm here. I should also add that she has told him you will not speak to him alone under any circumstances." The words 'visitor' and 'him' are delivered in a way that indicates Mrs Baker does not think much of him. She adds, "It's completely up to you, I can wait if you like, give you a minute or two to talk to your mum before you decide."

"Who is this visitor?" asks Grace.

"An American," came the non-specific reply. Unhelpful, but delivered with the same hint of condescension she had used previously.

Grace looks at Syd, who shrugs.

"Why not? Will you both come with me?" She looks at Grace, who says yes, then me. I am not sure why she wants me there, perhaps she thinks my previous experience will stand me in good stead. I'm not convinced about that – but don't say so. Whatever, if I can help I will. I nod.

"Okay, thank you. I'll let the boss know."

After Mrs Baker has bustled back out of the room Grace turns to Syd,"Are you sure? You don't have to."

"I want to if it will help sort this mess out, thanks for saying you'll come with me."

"I wouldn't let you go on your own, whatever this mess is we're all in it together now."

They hug, and I feel kind of left out, until Syd comes over and embraces me too. I see Grace smile at me over her shoulder.

"I know you didn't need to be here, but I'm glad you are."

I flinch inwardly, knowing how close I had come to just walking away and leaving my demons safely boxed up. It was mainly the promise of being 'off the hook' with Alice that had persuaded me, not altruism or bravery. Even so, I'm glad I am here, although it is not necessarily for the right reasons.

"Me too, it'll all work out in the end you know."

"I hope so."

We retreat to our respective chairs again, resuming our silent contemplation and wondering what will happen next. I can't tell what the others are thinking, and am afraid to ask. My mind is whirling with possibilities, the fact that this 'meeting' might not go the way we want it to, the uncertainty of what is going to happen when this is over, the chance that I might get to make another go of it with Grace. This time I would get things right, this time I would step up and be the man I should have been twenty five years ago. Only, I know myself too well, I'm not sure if I'm brave enough to do what needs to be done before my resolve fails, like it did before.

The door opens again and Alice steps in. Her face is unreadable, but it is definitely not the friendly smile from a few days ago. She is accompanied by a tall man with cropped blond hair. He is wearing jeans, a ridiculous pair of cowboy boots and a plain white tee shirt. He is unremarkable in every way, apart from a fresh, ugly bruise around his eye and a gap where one of his front teeth should have been lining up with the rest of his dazzlingly white smile. He strides confidently into the room and takes one of the vacant chairs. Alice waits by the door for a moment, collecting a fresh tray of hot tea and coffee from Mrs Baker before coming over to join us.

The next few minutes are taken up with the pouring of drinks, which the American impatiently declines. Eventually we run out of trivial things to cover our nervousness, the activity stops and as we settle all eyes turn to the American. He is at one end of the table, now strewn with games, Uno cards, coffee pots and mugs, we are at the other end, Alice sitting slightly away from us. Syd has positioned herself between myself and Grace. Or did we put her there to protectively flank her? I honestly couldn't say.

Syd and Grace both have furrowed brows and straight mouths, I attempt what is intended to be a reassuring smile in Syd's direction but I'm not sure it amounts to much. Alice is her usual composed self, she looks as though she is about to speak, but before she can say anything the American beats her to it, "It's good to finally meet y'all in person."

His smile does not get beyond his mouth, everyone else looks at me and I realise, belatedly, that his piercing green eyes are directed solely at me.

"Eh?" I reply, and I wish it had been something pithier, because now I am unexpectedly the centre of attention. I wish I had some response other than the semi-grunted, high-pitched surprised noise I had made.

"Oh yeah, we've been interested in you for a long time. Since you and your friends got everyone worked up in eighty six, I kept hoping you'd come for a visit to the good old US of A – I knew you'd be back in the picture eventually."

I make a similar stupid sound to the one I had made previously and look helplessly to Alice. She looks momentarily puzzled, as though she has lost some of her composure, she swiftly regroups and answers on my behalf, "He's nothing to do with this, he's just here as a favour to me."

That might have been true at the start, now I'm not so sure, but I'm not going to contradict her.

"Well, he's here now, so that makes him something to do with it. I had a hunch he would lead us somewhere interesting if we waited long enough, much easier thanks to that lovely phone you provided him with - thanks. Anyway, I was right, wasn't I?"

The way he is talking makes me glad I never had been for a trip to 'the good old US of A'. I get the distinct impression from what he has just said that he, or someone like him, would have put on quite a reception for me. I look to Alice who does a thing with her eyebrow, as if to say 'I've no idea' in answer to my unasked question. The moment is fleeting, the American turns his attention to Syd.

"I think you have something of ours." He fixes her with his stare and she shrinks back into the chair.

"She doesn't, she has nothing," Grace replies on Syd's behalf.

"Well, I reckon she does. I think it would be best to make sure eh?" he responds.

There is a brief silence before Alice, now fully back in the game, breaks it – her voice searing precisely and authoritatively across the table, "What, exactly, do you think she has?"

"She's been looking at things that don't belong to her, I need to know what she knows."

"I don't know anything.," Syd replies, "I didn't do anything it was…"

Before she can finish Alice interrupts, "I told you, she's not the person you're looking for. She has nothing, she knows nothing."

"Then how come it was her computer, in her flat, that's been snooping around our secure servers?"

"How could you possibly know that? Who's been giving you your information?"

Alice

She knows he won't answer, not fully anyway. He's just fishing, hoping to get Syd to say something – anything – that will tell him he's on the right track. He isn't, but she's not about to let him know that just yet, you don't play all your best cards at once. Besides, she has some angling of her own to take care of.

Right now this situation feels like the plot of a Dickens novel, strewn with unlikely coincidences and random twists of fate. She had no idea that she wasn't the only one who had continued to monitor the events of 1986, or how he would have got that level of detailed information.

This summer had been long and busy, all the centres had been fully occupied with the organisers and agitators that had been coordinating the riots which had spread from city to city across the UK. Trying to keep a lid on things and stop it carrying on into the autumn had been everybody's main priority. Out of the public eye ringleaders had been gathered up, bought in and given some time to think things over before getting an opportunity to start again.

Her last 'customer' had been extraordinarily cooperative and had been moved on quickly. So when the hacking of the CIA database had come to light, through a random and fortuitous flag in her services own routine monitoring, they were the only centre that had capacity to manage it. Once Syd had been identified the first thing Alice had done was to look through Syd's background checks. She thought she recognized Grace's name and following a hunch had traced the links back to 1986. Mrs Baker had got the old files out, but Alice couldn't see any connection between the two events other than sheer coincidence.

She had never really thought she would have to contact him again, her sporadic observations had been more through curiosity than caution - and had been waning over recent years anyway. But he was one of her first success stories and it had been satisfying to see him flourishing and thriving. His case had stayed with her to the extent that when O'Brien, her old boss, retired, she stepped into his shoes –

partly due to her memories of that incident and the difference she had been able to make. She hadn't intended to, she had already carved a niche for herself in the foreign office when O'Brien had invited her back into the fold.

After years of living out of a suitcase, being flown from city to city and enduring stuffy dinners with diplomats and foreign officials she had grown tired of what had looked glamorous from the outside but turned out to be quite mundane. Mostly it was massaging the egos of men who weren't used to being told 'no'.

She had initially been surprised when O'Brien had contacted her to say he had put her name forward as his possible successor. After taking a day or two to reflect she saw it made sense. She had been good at what she did and realised then that she missed working at the centre. She had taken the role on, with his blessing.

The fact that the American was so well informed about past and present events came as a surprise to her, later she would have questions about how come she wasn't told, or - if nobody knew - why the hell not? What did make sense now was the phone; if the American had access to the tracking app it would have led him straight to wherever he needed to be. All he had to do was follow the phone, it had been set up so that the phone didn't even need to be switched on. It was the same way that she had made contact. She wondered how he had piggy-backed onto a bespoke and top secret piece of software, and why it hadn't been picked up. More questions for later. Maybe it shouldn't really be a surprise though, the recent endemic of phone hacking by the tabloids had woken everybody up to how public their private information actually was.

Right now she wanted to see how much information she could harvest from this situation. The American had already let her know how worried the top ranks were by turning up in person, unannounced, twice. An act that would normally be unthinkable in their circles. He had also confirmed her suspicion that they already knew more about her centre than was healthy, not entirely surprising after the amount of time they had been operating here. But even so, a wake-up call that it was time to reboot their system – start afresh.

The other centres would need to be alerted of course, all in good time though.

She was assuming that the American still didn't know about Rick yet. Or, more importantly, that he was here at the centre already. It was an ace she was keeping firmly up her sleeve until there was no longer a reason to withhold it. Once that information was out the game would change again, she wanted to make sure she had time to get ready.

Now it was time for her to turn the screw a little, she probed about what it was they were looking for – and why they thought Syd would have been able to download whatever it was. She offered him Syd's laptop for his team to dissect (her own tech guys had already got everything there was to get) and asked him about why this was so important and what he thought Syd might be able to tell him.

He gave away nothing, not that she expected him to. He merely repeated that some 'sensitive information' had been accessed and that they just needed to check what Syd had seen. The fact that he kept stonewalling her, and that he was here in the first place, exposed this lie. They both knew this, and each knew that the other knew it too.

Her tech guys had not found anything on the laptop, but the sprinkling of clues they had collected from other agencies' intelligence gathering hinted strongly towards activity in the Middle East. With the recent events occurring in Tunisia and Morocco spreading to Egypt, it wasn't too big a leap of the imagination to guess that the sensitive information was linked in some way to the Arab Spring. How and why was not certain, but again an educated guess would be that America had been trying to destabilise the area by facilitating the unrest, bringing about a new order in the region. The why, of course, would be oil – it always came down to oil in the end.

She tried to convince the American, again, that they did not have the hacked files and did not know where they were. Any pretence of ambiguity was dropped, both acknowledging tacitly that the other knew perfectly well that it was about a data breach. As far as she was concerned this prevarication was ideal, it gave her colleagues time to talk to Rick and dismantle his flat. Teams of experts were on both these jobs even as they spoke. She was sorry it was prolonging things for Syd, but it was the way it had to be.

Her last brief conversation with Carl had been an update on how the search of the flat was going. According to him, the flat now resembled a construction site, the crew were systematically checking every item of furniture, fixture, fitting and appliance, he thought they were going to start taking the ceilings down next. Although she knew he was joking about this, she also knew that they wouldn't stop until they had investigated, unscrewed and dismembered everything in the flat. They were tenacious and would not quit until they had found something, or were certain there was nothing to find. Until then she would stall the American for as long as she possibly could. She looked around the room at the worried expressions of her visitors, then at the smug self-assured face of the American. She wished again that she had got Carl to put him in the boot of the car before they left the farm. Inwardly sighing she launched into another time-wasting round of unanswered questions.

Rick

He hadn't been too worried at first, confident that once he was in a police cell, lawyers would be appointed and he would be able to disappear to wherever his superiors wanted him to go. He had never anticipated the possibility of being transported to some covert facility where the rules did not apply.

He hadn't been badly treated, but the reality of his situation was beginning to dawn on him. Until now it had all been a bit of a lark, some mischief making and a chance to disrupt some corrupt, morally bankrupt western governments. Also, as it turned out, a chance to get laid. The assurances of his friends and handlers, that he would be safe and looked after, seemed empty right now.

After being delivered to the building on the moors he was left in a small bare room, amounting to little more than a windowless cell, which is what it was. The grandmotherly old lady who had directed him wordlessly to the room had appeared incongruous next to the armed guard who accompanied her. He had tried his best charm offensive on her, smiling and looking vulnerable at the same time.

"Where am I, what's going to happen?"

"Shut the fuck up and get in the room, before I tell him to knock some of your teeth out."

She motioned to the guard who stepped forward even as Rick was retreating into the room. The door closed and locked and that was when he finally admitted to himself that he really was in trouble.

In the eternity before anything else happened he sat on the bed, running through possible scenarios in his head. Escape didn't seem to be an option, he was fairly sure they weren't going to kill him, he clearly wasn't destined for a courtroom anytime soon and he doubted that they would torture him – which meant they wouldn't be able to get him to tell them where the flash drive was. Without that they had nothing, so surely they would have to let him go, wouldn't they?

Another woman, younger this time, had come into the room. She was alone and seemed relaxed as she leaned against the wall opposite him. He eyed the door which she had left ajar. Following his gaze she shook her head slightly.

"Don't bother, there's nowhere to go and you're on camera. The first sign of anything untoward will end very unpleasantly, I guarantee it."

"What if I take you hostage?"

This elicited a laugh that made him feel foolish and angry at the same time.

"Go ahead, try it."

"I want my phone call and I want a lawyer, I know my rights."

This got another display of amusement.

"You really haven't figured out how deep the shit is yet have you? What did you think was going to happen? Did you think our national security was going to turn a blind eye?"

"I still have rights though."

"Not here you don't." This was delivered in such a calm, flat, matter-of-fact way that he was in absolutely no doubt that it was true.

"We've got a lot of questions for you, and you're going to answer them. Let's start with where's the flash drive?"

"What flash drive?"

"Ah, that could be a problem, it's not the answer I wanted. So let's try again, flash drive?"

"I told you..."

"Never mind, we'll find it. You don't seem to be getting the idea of this though, so let me explain it simply; nobody knows you're here. Hell, even people who work here don't know you're here. We can keep you here indefinitely, as long as it takes for you to start cooperating."

"Somebody will..."

"No, nobody will. The only good thing that can happen now is you tell us what we need to know, then tell us how to contact your handler so they can take you away. We'll be sure to let them know you cooperated fully, which they'll be delighted about."

"How's that good?"

"Okay, I'll admit it wouldn't be that good for you, but it would give me a huge amount of satisfaction. There is one other alternative."

She paused and looked at him, letting him know she was offering him a lifeline. He took the bait.

"What's that?"

"You cooperate with us, we don't need much from you - you're small fry. Give us enough to catch a big fish or two, maybe even a shark, then we'll throw you back. We'll even give you a new identity - if we have a good haul."

"Not going to happen."

"I guessed you'd say that, but I thought I'd offer anyway." She smiled, and there was something deeply unsettling about that perfectly ordinary expression. Maybe the every-day nature of it, maybe the knowledge that it hid something else, something calculating and threatening.

"Anyway, I've got things to do. I'll leave you to think about it for a bit."

She left and the door closed again, he was alone in the silent, empty room once more. It was an oppressive, almost aggressive silence. With no way of measuring the time that was passing Rick sat and watched the blinking lights of the cameras mounted in the ceiling and tried to think his way out of his situation.

There was no way he would cooperate with them of course – well not ordinarily anyway. But right now he was getting scared, he believed what the woman had told him – both about nobody knowing he was here and the possibility of them keeping him here indefinitely. He also wondered if he had been a bit hasty in ruling out the possibility of being tortured. Maybe if he did tell them what they wanted to know he could start over and do something more ordinary and productive with his life, stop having to look over his shoulder all the time.

Although, he hadn't even been looking over his shoulder that well apparently. He thought he had covered his tracks so completely, been so careful. Now all he wanted was a way out, preferably one that wouldn't involve him getting hurt too much, and regain his freedom. He couldn't see how it could get any worse, until it did.

The door opened and the old woman came in and placed a plate and a mug on the table. He was pretty sure there would be someone with a gun or a baton standing somewhere close nearby.

"Food and drink," she said succinctly, "we're not monsters you know."

There was a slight smile as she said this, then the door was closed. He picked up the plate and examined a plain cheese sandwich, no mayo, just two slices of bread, margarine and a slice of cheddar. Next he picked up the mug and sniffed the brown liquid, coffee. At least he had coffee, he momentarily perked up, then he sipped it and tasted it for what it was, cheap instant coffee, which he forced himself to drink because he was thirsty.

CHAPTER 17
Night

The meeting seemed to go on forever, with little or no input from me, Grace or Syd after the initial introductions. The American and Alice fired questions and counter-questions at one another, with neither seeming to actually answer anything. It reminds me of a school staff meeting, one of those tedious ones when something is discussed, debated and dissected for a full hour and everyone and his uncle has something to say about it. Finally a stalemate is reached and everyone agrees that they should keep things exactly as they were at the start.

I lose concentration and look across at Grace, whose eyes are fixed on Syd, they are both listening intently. Syd still looks worried, putting on a mask of bravado that can't hide the slightly haunted and hunted look she has been wearing since I met her, and I think she's right to be worried. As I see it, her future is hanging in the balance, the difference between going about her normal life or spending it too scared to act or move forward – like me.

I am sure that Alice is not going to give up on her easily, I don't know her well, but I have known her for a long time. I want to say this to Syd and Grace, to tell them that Alice will go all out to make this right. I have no way of doing this right now, so I have to let it go.

I think about this morning as I look at Grace, a frown of concentration and worry on her features. I remember how she looked before the years crept up on us. She was beautiful then, and the time between had added an extra layer to her face, if anything even more beautiful than in her youth. I wish I could say the same for myself, but am aware of the grey in my hair, the bags appearing under my eyes and the slight paunch that I see when I look down.

I'm trying to decide what it meant, if it meant anything at all or had just been for comfort or for old times sake. I hope it was more than that, but my mind is finding it hard to take in everything that has happened – that is still happening. I am still chasing these thoughts around my head when the American stands up. I realise, belatedly, that Alice has suggested a break. I am not sure why she has suggested this as I had missed that part of the conversation, but I am glad of the chance to stretch my legs and use the loo.

I go outside and light a cigarette – yes, I asked Mrs Baker for some more, which she procured without comment or judgement. What can I say? It's this place. I slump down to sit on the path, with my back against the bare concrete wall which gives me some shelter from the breeze. Outside the pool of yellow light that surrounds the centre it is now pitch dark, I can see two guards at the gatehouse – both in flak jackets and wearing helmets. Another pair come into sight as they round the corner on a never ending tour of the perimeter. One pauses and turns his torch towards me, dazzling me and making me look away before he moves on.

Syd comes out, looks across to where I am sitting, then comes over and sits next to me. She lowers herself to the floor far more nimbly and gracefully than I had done earlier.

"You hate it here, don't you?"

"Yep, is it that obvious?"

"And then some."

"It doesn't have good memories for me."

"Me neither now, I guess we've got that in common eh?"

"I guess."

I stub my cigarette, my mouth feels dry and it tastes bitter. I don't move to get up.

"I'm sorry this has happened to you."

"Yeah, it's not fair on you either, will you go home when this is over?"

I understand what she is asking, and don't answer immediately. After a few seconds I reply,

"I don't know, I'll need to sort some things out, but I think it's time to move on."

Now that I've said it out loud I feel like I've made a decision, after years of inertia – and cowardice. I've put my life on hold for decades, I don't know if me and Grace have another chance, but fate has thrown us back together and I don't want to make the same mistake twice.

"Mum will be pleased, she likes you. You've bought back some of the smiles that have been missing since Dad fucked off."

Before she has chance to say more Grace and Alice join us in the chilly darkness. Grace does her teacher voice, "What are you two doing out here?"

We reply simultaneously, "Nothing."

"He was smoking."

"Snitch", I tap her leg with the back of my hand and she pretends I have mortally wounded her, rubbing it and grimacing.

"Anyway," I say, "It's only a temporary thing."

"Good, it's disgusting." Grace smiles as she says this, but I get the point. I also enjoy the smile, her face lights up, even in the dark – if that makes sense.

Alice interjects.

"We need to go back in now, but not for long. I'm going to suggest we finish up for tonight, buy us some more time. It's going well."

"Is it?" Syd asks.

"Yes, tomorrow will wrap things up. I've still got some more things to do tonight, but I'm pretty sure we'll have everything we need to sort things out."

Nobody replies, I look at Alice trying to gauge if this was to placate Syd and Grace or if things really are going well. My mind snaps back to a train platform in 1987. I had the same thoughts then, was Alice bluffing, or did she have things under control? That afternoon she had calmly and quietly laid out the options – clearly and in full command of the situation. It had scared me slightly then, but I realise that I have never known Alice to not be in control, even on days like yesterday when it all changed so quickly and everything happened at once. She seemed to have a plan for everything. Her all-encompassing web of intelligence, backups, and good judgement made her like a spider sitting in the middle of a web. I can see it in her eyes now, reassuring and calm, safe in the knowledge that she has the upper hand. I can see Grace and Syd coming to the same conclusion and try to smile reassuringly as I resign myself to another night at the centre.

I start to struggle to my feet, Grace offers her hand. I take it, soft and warm, and push myself upwards and forwards with her assistance. I make a slight grunting noise that hides the sound of my knees popping. Syd has already sprung to her feet and is going inside with Alice.

There are no double beds here. Grace and I briefly discuss the option of sharing a single and both decide it would be preferable to sleeping alone. I am sure Grace can feel my discomfort and this is an act of charitable sympathy on her part. Nevertheless I am grateful. I yawn loudly, it has been a long day. Grace returns the yawn as she strips down to her underwear – I don't know if she doesn't know or is just past caring about the camera in the corner, probably the latter. We climb into the tiny bed. The light in the room fades, leaving white light from the corridor spilling through the crack where I have left the door slightly ajar. It illuminates Grace's face and I watch her as she settles, then I fall asleep with my arms wrapped around her.

I dream of home, except – as is the way in dreams – nothing was quite right. My parents did not recognise me and all my friends and acquaintances were chasing me through the deserted streets for no discernible reason. I woke in a panic and held Grace tighter before eventually falling back asleep.

Alice

Inside the perimeter, in a whirling conflagration of bright lights and noise, Carl's black clad figure emerged from the maelstrom and walked briskly, bent slightly, towards the building. Alice was waiting outside the door, her hair blowing in the tempest created by the blades of the helicopter as it departed. She clutched her cardigan around her, as much to keep it from flapping around her as to ward off the cold night air. They shouted greetings to each other as she led the way inside the building, leaving the noise and darkness behind them, directly to the brightly lit climate-controlled space of her office.

She poured a fresh cup of coffee for Carl as he made himself comfortable in one of the chairs facing her desk, she carried the mug over and put it down in front of him. Picking up her own drink from her desk and cupping it in her hands she took the seat opposite him, then looked up at him expectantly.

His smile took over his face and lit up his eyes as he reached into his pocket, pulling out a nondescript, black box – only slightly bigger than a phone, that he placed on the desk in exchange for his drink. He blew across the top of his mug then slurped noisily.

"You took your time." This is said with a smile, Alice is delighted that Carl has not come back empty-handed.

"Don't blame me, the search team faffed around all day." This is also delivered with a wry grin, it is an in-joke where everybody slopey-shoulders the blame to the next person when things have taken longer than they would have wanted.

"Where was it?"

"Do you remember Jim?"

She does, she has worked with him many times. He is one of the best forensics search guys on the team.

"Yes, where was it?"

"I'm telling you. After they had unscrewed all the light fittings and socket plates and dismantled all the furniture he got the team to disassemble all the appliances. Everyone else started with the usual suspects – TV, X-box, radio. Jim decided to start in the kitchen, so he eventually got round to the coffee maker – Jackpot. It was slid into a space behind the switch panel. God knows how he even saw it, it just looked like part of the workings – but he did, he's a legend!"

"Remind me to buy Jim a drink sometime. Is it definitely what we're looking for?"

"I bloody hope so, Jim's busy getting the flat back to its original state, I don't want to be the one to tell him to start ripping it apart again. Anyway, nobody's had a look yet, I bought it straight here. I guess you're going to get Bob out of bed to decrypt it now?"

"I don't think Bob's gone to bed yet, he's too busy playing with the other presents you sent him."

"Yeah, sounds like Bob, I bet he's like a pig in shit. I'll take it down to him in a moment shall I?."

"That would be good, thanks, and thanks for today, it was a good job."

"All part of the service. How's the kid bearing up?"

"She's doing okay, they all are. Nobody's freaked out or shut down. I hope I've called this right – for their sakes."

"For what it's worth I'd have done the same, Ma'am, I think it's fallen well for us so far. I like that kid though, she's really kept her cool."

He took a larger swig of his coffee and shifted forward, moving to get up.

"Ah, before you go there's something else."

Carl settles back into his chair and drinks some more of his coffee,

"Of course there is," he smiled.

"The visitor that you dealt with yesterday."

"The American? Did we collect him?"

"Not exactly, he turned up here under his own steam. His team must have gotten to the farm first. He arrived early this evening demanding to talk to Syd."

"Here? At the centre?"

"Yes, it's confirmed my suspicions that I spoke to you about at the farm."

"Ah shit, a leak is all we need. What did you tell him anyway? Or did you just shoot the fucker?"

"He said he just wanted to talk to her. I trust him as far as I can throw him, but I don't think he knows as much as he's pretending."

"So the leak's down the food chain then? Do you want me to beat him up again?"

"No, well not yet anyway. He's coming back tomorrow morning. We should have had time to finish talking to Rick, and unpacking that hard drive by then. He's getting to be a bit of a nuisance, Bob's dug up some info on him. I'd like you to have a look through it, so you're familiar with who he is and how he operates. It may be useful to know."

"Will do, anything else?"

"Stay on your toes, I've got no idea where we're leaking from, it could be anybody. Now, go and get some rest."

"Yes, Ma'am."

Carl picked up the rectangular black box and left. Alice drank from her coffee mug and leant back in the chair with her eyes closed and a trace of a smile on her face.

Rick

The time passed neither quickly or slowly, it just passed. He sat and did calculations in his head, trying to work out what he could offer that they wanted without compromising himself. He knew that the flash drive was what they wanted right now, they had made that clear, maybe if they had that they would be more open to negotiation. He made up his mind that he would tell them where it was, if they would let him contact someone and start to work out how to leave.

Foul coffee and mediocre snacks were delivered at intervals, the times felt random to Rick, probably to make sure he didn't try to estimate the amount of time that was passing. The lights stayed on permanently and the silence became a palpable thing, his blood beating in his veins and the slight rustle of his movements as the only sounds. It was oppressive and discomforting, leading to him talking to himself out loud to break the silence. As he articulated his thoughts it never once occurred to his genius level brain that the cameras would be recording every word he spoke as well as his movements.

He was just leaning back and closing his eyes when there was a bang on the door and it opened. He sat up as the same man who had come bursting into his flat stepped into the room. He walked over and sat next to him on the bed, too close to be comfortable, but he had nowhere else to go. He felt the bulk and presence of the man next to him, solid and immovable.

"Hello again."

"I'll tell you where it is if you get in touch with my contact for me," Rick blurted out.

"What, the flash drive?"

"Yes."

"Funny thing, I'm pretty sure you don't know where it is. If you wanted to tell me that it used to be inside the coffee machine, I'm not that interested."

Rick's heart sank, he had thought he had one good bargaining chip, now he was back to square one. His mind raced, thinking what else he could offer next to show he was cooperating. He could tell them about Abasi and how to get in touch with him, maybe even tell them the small amount he'd been able to find out using his not inconsiderable computer skills.

"I can tell you about the group."

Carl raised his eyebrows.

"I can tell you the name of my contact and how to get in touch with him."

Now a shark-like grin rose to the surface of Carl's face,

"Another funny thing, you're not the only computer hacker in the world you know. Our tech guy, he's good, tells me you've left a considerable amount of useful information for him on your laptop. I know, it was encrypted and password protected and you used VPRs, but like I said, he's good."

Any kind of purchase Rick thought he might have was being taken from him. He frantically thought about what he could do next. His deliberations were interrupted again.

"The thing is, you did a bad thing to someone who I've got to know a little over the last couple of days. You hurt her and got her into a lot of trouble, and my priority right now is to keep her safe and help get her out of that trouble. Trust me, if I thought that kicking you black and blue would help I'd do it, in the blink of an eye."

Rick believed him, there was nothing threatening or aggressive in the way it had been said, which was, paradoxically, what made him certain that this man was more than capable of carrying out the afore mentioned beating – and maybe more.

"Anyway, I'll let you think about that for a while. Someone will bring you some more coffee in a bit," he smirked, "until then sit tight. My boss will come back and let you know what might be happening later. I kind of hope it's the beating black and blue thing, but that's not really her style unfortunately." He grinned and clapped Rick on the shoulder as he stood up to leave, making him flinch. "Still, always a first time eh?"

Night (continued)

I emerge into the strange muffled silence of the morning, Grace's gentle breathing is amplified in the tiny room and she is wrapped around me. I try to move gently, so as not to wake her, but I am unsuccessful. She pulls me towards her and hugs me tightly.

"Don't go, I'm not ready for the day to start yet."

"Me neither, but I need the loo."

"I suppose so, go on then."

She releases me so I can get to the little bathroom cubicle. The room gradually lightens, the penumbra is replaced by the bright glow of electric lights and the day begins – at least in this small part of the centre. Grace replaces me in the tiny bathroom and soon we are both dressed and leaving in search of tea and coffee, which we locate in the meeting room.

Syd and Alice are already waiting for us, Syd raises her eyebrows at us over the top of her coffee mug and the corners of her mouth turn into a smile as she sips. She says nothing, because she doesn't need to. She is sitting on the chair with her legs tucked underneath her and is wearing a baggy, yellow jumper that she has procured from somewhere. Grace and I are still in the crumpled clothes that we had hastily put on yesterday, I am glad that there was fresh underwear – but I feel like I could do with a proper change of clothes. Grace detours around the table on her way to collect a drink and puts her hand on Syd's shoulder.

"Morning, sweetness, did you sleep okay?"

"I suppose – you?"

"I'll sleep better when we get back to our own house, we all will."

She looks at Alice as she makes the last comment, Alice looks up from the screen of her laptop and smiles. She is immaculately turned out, as always, grey trousers and a red shirt – or is it a blouse? I never know the difference. Anyway, the smile is reassuring and it tells me that whatever the day brings Alice will have everything in hand.

"It'll be fine," she says. "Is everyone ready?"

I'm not really, I finish my toast and cradle my cup of tea as I take a seat next to Grace, then wait to see what is going to happen next.

Carl comes into the room. I'm a little surprised to see he is wearing a suit and tie. He holds the door for the American, who is accompanying him, both men appear to keep a wary distance from one another. The American scans the room, taking in the surroundings that are largely unchanged from last time we were here, someone has tidied the clutter and cleaned up while we slept. Carl's eyes stay firmly on the American – only flickering away briefly to acknowledge Alice and us as the American takes a chair facing us, then Carl steps back and stands by the wall, still watching, his hands folded loosely in front of him.

"Okay, you've kept me waiting long enough. I really need to spend some time with this child. If you cannot accommodate that things will escalate in the upstairs rooms, my superiors are not happy that you are holding out on us."

"Maybe your superiors, and you, would like to stop bullshitting and get to the point."

The American does not respond to this, a tiny shrug - maybe, an almost imperceptible quizzical lift of his eyebrow and a very long pause before Alice continues.

"We know what you want, and why you want it. I can tell you categorically that 'the child' does not have it, she has no knowledge or information about your government's involvement in the build up to the events in Tunisia, or anything that happened after that. She is not the person you are looking for. I would say, this is a lost cause, sooner or later the truth will be out there anyway – but it won't come from here, or from her. Wikileaks already seems to have an inside track to the Pentagon anyway."

There is another lengthy pause. The American opens his mouth to speak, but before he can say anything Alice interrupts,

"So, cards on the table, this is what we want. Syd is ours, she is now, and will be going forward, under our protection. She is off-limits to you, this is non-negotiable." She glances at me then adds, "You will not hack her phone, look at her e-mails, contact her or her friends and family or access any of her personal records."

"Why in hell would I agree to that?"

"Because she never saw what was taken – but we know who did. We've even seen it ourselves now. In return for you leaving her alone we will give you the hacker. This is the only deal you get. Turn it down and we'll keep it all, but it makes sense to me that you'd want the person who actually took your information rather than this unfortunate young lady, who was just in the wrong place at the wrong time."

The mention of Rick seemed to make the American's composure falter slightly, he quickly returns to his default smug.

"You think you know where this mysterious hacker is do you?"

"Yes, he's right here. Go and speak to your superiors, tell them the deal, then, once they've agreed, you can take him away with you."

"How did you…?"

"Mostly thanks to the brave and determined young woman you seem so intent on pursuing and harassing, now go and tell your bosses to leave her alone."

"Give me 10." He gets up and leaves the room with Carl escorting him out. He seemed genuinely surprised by this turn of events and was clearly not prepared for them, glancing back over his shoulder as he left.

The door clicks closed and Syd asks, "Is that it? As easy as that? What will happen to Rick?"

"Well, I wouldn't exactly say that any of this was easy would you? But yes, I think that will be it. Rick will go with him and answer all their questions. When he's done that he'll answer them all again, and then again until they are satisfied they can't get anything else out of him. Then they'll trade him in and get back one of their own people."

"Will they keep their side of the bargain? Will they leave Syd alone?" I ask.

"We've had Rick for 24 hours now. Once they know that, they'll know that we have had time to ask him questions of our own, the fact that we have some of the answers gives us a good deal of insurance. They really don't want their dirty laundry out for everyone to see."

"Did he say why it was me?" Syd asked.

"He said you were 'convenient', his job was to spread dissent and distrust between us and America, by any means necessary. You just happened to be the first person he came across who could help him achieve that. If it wasn't for you he would have undoubtedly moved on to another victim on another campus somewhere, his bag was already packed when he was collected."

"Bastard," Syd looks simultaneously angry and dejected.

"I'm sorry, if I could I'd let Carl have five minutes to teach him some manners, but it's not really the done thing."

"Will that really be it then?" I ask, changing the subject.

"I think so, they don't have any viable options apart from taking the deal. Now, who wants some more tea?"

The rest of the day is kind of a blur. I get the sense that there is more horse trading going on behind the scenes that we don't know about, but I don't see the American again. There is a lot of hanging about while Alice comes in and out making reassuring noises but giving us little in the way of actual information.

I have just picked up another six cards to add to my dismal Uno hand – we've started another lacklustre game, but our hearts aren't in it. Grace is distracted and Syd is only giving it lip-service. Even so, they are still beating me soundly. I am fighting the temptation to go outside to smoke, to stem the boredom – so far I am resisting.

Our recent movements have left us short of personal belongings, mostly what we are standing in is what we've got, although even that is not quite true. Grace and I were provided with navy blue hoodies and plain tee shirts during the day, while our own clothes were taken away to be laundered. We still have some belongings, but it is a limited selection, mostly we are in things we have managed to collect along the way. The only one of us who seems to have come out of it well is Syd in her yellow jumper. She has it cinched with a belt at the middle and a red scarf tying back her hair. Grace mentioned it, questioning her as to how come she had got all the extras and nice bits, her answer was simple.

"I asked."

I feel a pang of guilt as I realise that Grace is the newbie here, that she hasn't experienced first-hand the ease with which requests seem to be accommodated here at the centre. I have passed Mrs Baker's office several times and seen Syd in there talking to her, I even heard the older woman laughing once. It's not what you know….

Alice's head and shoulders appear around the edge of the door, providing a welcome distraction from the game I have almost lost.

"Can you come with me? You might want to see this."

She waits a moment for us to follow, then leads us out of the doors overlooking the car park. A cold wind is cutting across the open space and clouds are swooping over, looking for places to unload their liquid cargo. As we arrive the American appears around the far corner of the building. His long coat is being whipped around his legs by the wind, and behind him is a disconsolate looking young man, who I assume is Rick. As we watch Syd shouts across the empty space, "Oi!"

Both men turn to look in time to see her making a most unladylike gesture with the middle digits of both hands. There is no acknowledgement from either of them, they just resume their trek towards the big black car. Alice beckons us back inside.

"Who was he?" I ask. "Who was he really?"

"Funnily enough, his name actually is Rick, but I can't really tell you any more than that."

"Where's he going?"

"I can't tell you that either, although to be truthful I'm not even 100% sure myself."

"Who was the American guy?"

By now we are back inside, Alice considers briefly, then answers, "A fucking idiot, if he thinks he can just turn up here and start telling us what to do. I'm holding on to his flash drive for now."

I wonder briefly why Alice would have shared that bit of information with us. Aside from the unexpected lapse in her professional demeanour, I wasn't sure why she would mention a flash drive. Syd was way ahead of me, "That's our insurance isn't it?"

"It is for now, yes. It will all be forgotten once the lid gets blown off the whole rotten thing, but until then, yes."

"So, can we go now?" Grace asks. She looks tired, seeing her like this makes me feel tired too.

"Soon, I'll ask Mrs B to start making the arrangements if you want to start gathering your things - what you've got left anyway. Your other belongings will all be collected and returned to you."

She leaves. I feel deflated now things are coming to an end. Syd's obscene gesture in the car park, satisfying as it was, felt anticlimactic. It also means I'm going back to the flat I've lived in for over 20 years, in the town I never really left. Same old job, same old everything. Part of me yearns for the safety and security of it, I wish Grace would come and join me. But the more pragmatic side of me knows that this is no more likely now than it had been when we were young.

Mrs Baker comes in and beckons to me to join her. Happy to be distracted, I follow her to her office where there is a new phone sitting in the middle of her desk, she holds out her hand,

"If you want to give me your old one I'll upgrade it. The tech team are really keen to have a look at yours. The new one is all set up for you – without any extras this time. Just a phone."

"Thanks," I reply. I fish the old one from my pocket and pass it over, then I pick up the new one from the desk and switch it on. It opens with my password and the home screen has all my usual icons over a picture of my parents, smiling ear to ear at their 40th wedding anniversary party. I look at it for a moment, then shake my head and ask, "Can you ask Alice if I can have a word with her please? I need to ask her for a favour."

Rick

The younger woman came back. After he had realised that the game was up he had met with her twice, each time answering all of her questions and giving up any and every bit of information that was asked of him, plus adding some extras that he hoped would earn him some brownie points. She smiled, but it was not a comforting smile. It was a smile that told him that whatever his fate was, it was already decided and out of his control, not that it had ever really been since he arrived here.

"Good news and not so good news," she announced, "which do you want first?"

Rick did not respond.

"Well, let's start with the good news then, we don't want you anymore, you can go."

She looked expectantly at him.

"So as far as I'm concerned you can leave here, and I hope I never see you again. The not so good news is that even though we're not interested it doesn't mean nobody else is."

She stepped aside from the doorway, making room for a tall blond man with a bruised eye. He smiled a gap-toothed smile and spoke, "You bet buddy, I've got some people who are really set on speaking to you. Hitch your horse."

He stepped back and beckoned for Rick to follow him as he started to turn.

"Go with him. It's better if you go under your own steam, less stressful all round. Enjoy your trip."

Rick stood slowly and did as he was told, knowing that he was about to be spirited away. He would become a non-person until they had finished with him, who knew when that would be. He had been scared before, now he was petrified, he looked at the woman pleadingly.

"You had your chance, you made your choices. Cooperate, like you did for us, and it might not go too badly. Goodbye."

The long walk to the car took place in silence, apart from Syd's shout across the car park. The American muttered 'classy' under his breath, as he led Rick on to the waiting car. Rick looked across at Syd and began to realise how much of a mistake he had made, how much he'd underestimated her and how badly he'd treated her. There would be more time to reflect on his poor choices he knew, lots and lots of time.

Syd

The next hour or two seem to drag and fly simultaneously. There really isn't much to get ready and Syd feels like she is all talked out for now. Evidently the others feel the same, they are both keeping their own council. Presumably, like her, they are thinking about what happens next. She assumes the arrangements from before would still be in place. Maybe that's for the best for now, she is coming round to the idea of a fresh start.

She is worried about Mum, this has been stressful for her too and she doesn't want her to go back to an empty house, her unfinished jigsaw puzzle and her never quite completed garden to dwell on things. It would be better if her uncle was around, but last time she saw him was for her grandad's funeral nearly four years ago. Since then there had been an ephemeral plan for them to visit him in New Zealand which had never come to fruition.

She is sure she will be staying at home for at least for another week or so, if not longer but she doesn't know what will happen after that. Grace had once confided in Syd that she thought Dad had been growing distant for some time. She felt she understood that feeling of betrayal a bit better now, she realises how much it must have hurt mum when he left her. She had, of course, been more focussed on her own grief to fully appreciate another person's point of view. When she spent a weekend with Dad and The Floozy they had not got on well. Far from fun, it had consisted mostly of awkward, forced smiles and everyone waiting until it was time for her to leave.

She hopes that Mum's old boyfriend will at least try to keep in touch, make some sort of an effort. It would help her peace of mind if her mum was not spending as much time on her own as she has been over the last year or so.

The ex seems to have mostly disappeared for the moment, probably reneging on his earlier promise and sneaking out for a crafty fag. She knows Mum is going to miss him when they leave. There is nothing she can do about any of these ifs, buts and maybes – there hasn't been for a while now in this shitshow. She just needs to wait and see what happens, then be ready to decide what the right thing to do is.

They have been offered some refreshments for the road by the attentive and well-organised Mrs Baker, a selection of snacks and drinks. She has loaded some into her bag, a tin of Coke, a couple of chocolate bars and some crisps, but what she really wants is to get back to their house and kitchen and help mum cook something with fresh veggies. Then they can sit and eat in the lounge, while they watch something crap, like that vampire thing on the TV – Trueblood. She is not entirely sure what day it is on or what time they will get back, not that it matters – it's crap on TV whatever night you watch it.

When Alice finally comes in to tell them all it's time to leave she feels a massive sense of relief, it washes over her like a wave. She can't imagine how it must feel for someone who was here for more than the short time she has experienced, and it looks like she's not going to find out as there are two cars ready to take them away, Carl is in one and Dan is standing by the other.

There are hugs and promises to be in touch again soon. The kind of made-to-be-broken promises that people often make after meeting up. Even at her tender age she is familiar with those. It's like when Dad said he would call her every week after he left. It was a mere three weeks before he forgot the first time. Weirdly, she feels a bit sad to be saying goodbye, she kind of likes Alice and mum's ex was alright. He is kind of funny and a bit sad, but okay. Not only that, but he had cheered Mum up in spite of the general shitness of the situation. She hoped he would be less flaky than Dad, but didn't have high hopes for that.

She had tried to talk to Mum, to ask if they would be staying in touch or meeting up again. Mum was kind of non-committal and vague, saying that she would wait and see what happened. Syd could see in her eyes that she was saying this to try and protect herself, to not get hurt again. Then she pushed a bit.

"You still like him though don't you?"

"Of course, we go back a long way."

"Then why don't you try to meet up again?"

"Because it's really up to him not me, he has a lot of things he needs to sort out. You know what happened to him, I think he's still struggling with that. He always has been."

"You could help him."

"How about you stop matchmaking and start getting ready to go?"

And that was it, but she could tell that Mum wanted it to carry on, that she really liked him, but the implication that it was none of her business was clear. She guessed time would tell.

Alice has come outside to say a cursory goodbye to everyone, she clearly has things she needs to get back to and joins in the farewells briefly, wishing everyone a safe journey before she goes back inside. Syd and Grace, carrying their meagre belongings with them, climb into Carl's car.

In this muted atmosphere, under a mass of yellow and grey clouds piling in from the distant hills, she settles into the car and they follow Dan's car through the open gate and onto the long straight road taking them away from the centre.

CHAPTER 18
Return

I am sitting next to Dan, our backs towards the grey concrete and high fences of the centre as it finally recedes behind us. I look back once and see Syd and Grace's car following as we reach the brow of the hill that will put the place out of sight once and for all. The relief I feel is only matched by my trepidation about going home, thinking about all the things that lie ahead of me, and worrying about when and how I am going to do them all. But all that is for later, for now I'm just focused on getting out of here.

As we start to ascend into the hills, large spots of rain begin to splash intermittently onto the windscreen, getting more frequent as we reach the rocky outcrop at the summit. The windscreen wipers make an audible clicking noise as they reach the nadir of their rhythmic sweeps of the glass, hypnotic and becoming more persistent as they speed up to match the growing intensity of the rain. Dan is taciturn and uncommunicative, he has been glancing in the rear view mirror constantly, presumably some security protocol he has to follow. He checks his watch once, then brings our car to such an abrupt and sudden halt that I am thrown forward against the seat belt as the car skids to a stop. I look ahead to see what has caused him to do this, peering through the rain at the unobstructed road ahead.

"Stay where you are!" he commands me as he unclips his seat belt, steps out of the car and turns towards the other car. I look back in confusion to see that they too are stationary, headlights on in the gloomy rain. Carl has kept a good distance between us in spite of Dan's emergency braking.

As I watch Dan reaches something from his hip, then points towards the other car. There are two muffled sounds, no louder than pops really, and one of the headlights of Carl's car winks out. I realise, belatedly, that Dan has fired shots at the car. I can't believe what I'm seeing, it's like something from Jason Bourne, I half expect the car to explode, or burst into flames, like they do on TV. I scramble with my seat belt and the car door, familiar actions that suddenly seem beyond my ability to master. Eventually I succeed in releasing myself and clamber out, the rain immediately flattens my hair to my scalp and the shoulders of my sweatshirt darken. I don't know what I thought I might achieve outside of the car, whatever it might have been I am quickly disabused of the notion that I might have any part of the proceedings. Dan turns and points the gun in my direction, I freeze – convinced he is going to shoot me.

He doesn't, he barks, "Get down on the fucking floor, face down, don't fucking move!"

I comply immediately, fearing for your life will do that for you. I practically throw myself on the cold, wet road in front of me, not caring how wet and dirty I am getting, not caring that I am doing nothing brave or helping Grace or Syd, right now I just don't want Dan to shoot me. I look up from my prone position in time to see Dan turn back and walk towards the other car with his arms outstretched in front of him. From where I am I can now see that the driver's door is open, it's hard to tell through the rain, but I think that the driver's seat is empty.

As Dan approaches the car, cautiously and slowly, I glimpse Carl. He is crouched behind the car, staying out of Dan's sightline. He is little more than a shadow, moving slowly around to keep the bulk of the vehicle between himself and Dan, who has reached the car and is putting his head inside to speak to Grace and Syd, the words are lost in the rain. The rear doors open and I panic. It is at this moment that I realise that I don't want to lose either of them, certainly not because of my cowardice and inaction. I get to my feet and take steps towards them as they are getting out of the car, I have no plan and no real expectation of overpowering Dan – I only know that I have to do something, anything.

While Dan is occupied with Grace and Syd, Carl rolls through the pooling water at the edge of the road and disappears down a short drop into the heather. Seconds later his head and shoulders reappear and he gesticulates for me to do the same, before ducking back down. I hesitate, not knowing if I have interpreted his signal correctly or not. I have no other plan, I look once more at Dan, who seems to have decided that I am not relevant and still has his back to me, then half roll, half fall into the drainage gulley at the side of the road. Where I was wet before, I am now soaking, laying in a pool of muddy water with singing grazes on the palms of my hands where I had hit the road heavily moments before.

I don't know what I am supposed to do now, I dare to put my head up enough to see Grace and Syd walking in front of Dan as he checks his watch again. Syd is closest to me, her tightly curled hair pulled straight by the rain and covering her eyes. She reaches to push it to one side and I see her grim expression in every part of her face. Grace is obscured by Syd, but I can picture the look on her face in my mind's eye, mirroring Syd and then adding some. Dan puts a cupped hand over his eyebrows and peers at the road ahead. In the distance a pair of rain blurred headlights appear, moving rapidly towards us. I duck down again as Dan scans the area, then look back up in time to see the car bearing down on us, the teeming raindrops glittering and flashing in the glare of its lights.

I am just deciding that I need to do something, even if it is just surrender. I brace myself to get up when a hand lands on my shoulder. It is all I can do to not scream, I flex and twist, landing in a deeper patch of mud and sliding further into the ditch. I turn and see Carl, one muddy finger pressed to his lips. I immediately feel calmer, I wasn't sure if somehow Dan had dispatched Carl when I was cowering in the ditch and I had missed it. Knowing that I am not the only one hiding in the dark makes me feel less spineless.

"What the fuck's going on?" I whisper.

"No time to chat, take this." He hands me a large knife, the kind that Rambo uses, one large serrated edge on top, a gleaming curve of blade underneath. I take it gingerly, not sure what he is expecting me to do with it. I'm not sure if I could stab someone, or cut their throat or anything like that, my experience as a primary teacher has left me ill-prepared for a situation like this, although I could probably have done some damage with a staple gun.

"Crawl along the edge, keep well down and don't let anyone see you. When the other car stops, see if you can take out one of its tyres. Anything you can do to disable it will help – and be careful. Go."

Phew, not killing people then. I follow my orders, not wanting to know what is going to happen behind me. I have seen that Carl has his pistol ready at his hip, I just hope that Grace or Syd are not going to get caught in any crossfire. I feel certain that Carl would not risk that, but even so a cold feeling sits deep in my stomach. I slide and slosh through the rain and mud, staying low in the gloom and pouring rain. Any remaining vestiges of dryness are now long gone, there is mud everywhere, I can feel it inside my clothes, in my hair and on my face. In the confusion I appear to have lost one of my shoes, I continue the short distance to where the approaching lights have now come to a halt. I look tentatively up, then hurriedly drop back down again as I see a familiar pair of cowboy boots and the dripping hem of a duster coat walk past me .

I crawl back up the side of the ditch and nervously look up again, to check he is gone. The coast is momentarily clear, I hunker down scared to move, what if…? The rain dripping down my back reminds me of that night in '86, the night of the storm – a quiet voice in the back of my mind asks simply 'what would Lisa do if she was here?'

This thought galvanizes me into action. If Lisa was here she would do what needed to be done, as she's not here it's going to fall to me. I raise myself into a crouch then scramble over the bank to the car, where I hunker beside the front wheel. I grip the wicked looking knife in my trembling hand, repeatedly looking in the direction of the American, certain he will have turned back and be bearing down on me. He hasn't and he isn't, I stab the blade towards the wall of the tyre. I had always assumed that this is a fairly straightforward thing to do, apparently it is not though. The knife glances off, gouging but not puncturing the tyre and nearly slipping out of my hand in the process. Swearing under my breath I take a firmer hold and try again, this time pushing as hard as I can with the point. It works, the blade sinks in and the tyre immediately deflates with a swoosh of warm air.

Now I have my next problem, I have pushed the knife in deep, the handle is wet and I am struggling to pull it out. I change my grip to below the hilt to get more leverage and immediately regret it as the keen blade slices into my fingers. I swear at my own stupidity, readjust my grip, then pull hard, nearly toppling backwards as the knife comes free. I scurry to the next wheel on shaking legs, glancing to try and see what is happening on the road ahead. I can see nothing from my low down position, through the dark and the rain. I repeat the previous process, only more efficiently now that I have perfected my technique, even with my injured hand it is easier this time. I make the executive decision to crawl around to the other side of the car, where I finish off the other two, the last one makes a satisfyingly loud popping noise as I force the knife into the wall of the tyre.

Emboldened, I stand up and look for Grace and Syd. Through the rain, in the sharp glare of the car headlights I can see three ghostly figures, I walk towards them with the knife held in my outstretched, bloodied hand, not sure what will happen as I approach, tensed as I half expect a shot to ring out with every step I take, but my body has produced enough adrenaline now to make me foolishly fearless. I can see two figures prostrate on the floor, but still can't make out who is who in the darkness. One is motionless, the other writhing in obvious pain.

As I continue to stumble forward one of the standing figures turns their head in my direction and starts to run towards me. I raise the knife reflexively, then lower it when I see it is Grace. I drop the knife and open my arms to embrace her as she bowls into me. I catch her and hold her, tightly, I'm never going to let her go again. Tears merge with the mud, rain and blood on my face and I feel two more, smaller, arms wrap themselves around both of us and I breathe a sigh of relief as I realise that Syd is safe too.

Looking over their shoulders I see Carl in the ghostly light of the car headlights. He has removed the laces from Dan's boots and is using them to truss the prone bodies of his two adversaries. He works fast and looks over to us as he is finishing off, he raises a thumb and shouts, "All okay?"

I manage to raise a thumb back, as I lift my hand I realise how much blood is pouring from my self-inflicted wound. Then the sound of thunder starts to rumble around us. No, not thunder, it's more insistent and increasing in intensity – becoming a roar.

Then all hell breaks loose. The whole area is suddenly flooded with an incandescent light from above that makes us lower our eyes, night turns to day and our shadows are clear and black on the rain soaked road. I look up as ropes fall from the sky, followed almost immediately by black clad ninja-style figures sliding down the lines at an impossible speed, landing on their feet, fully armed and crouching immediately into a protective circle around us, guns pointing outward. They run to various points in the area at an unheard command and carry out their designated duties. One comes to us and stands protectively between us and the central area between the cars, before ushering us towards the helicopter, which is now settling on the nearest section of flat land.

"What the fuck's going on? What's happening?" I shout to Grace before the helicopter, with us now safely on board, ascends vertically and follows the road back to the centre staying low to the ground. Grace mouths something back to me, but I can't hear her over the noise of the engines. She holds my muddy hand in hers – the one that is not currently being swaddled in a makeshift dressing provided by one of our ninja saviours – and mouths 'thank you', as she hugs Syd close with her other arm and the helicopter starts to descend after its brief flight.

I am shaking and crying, and cold – so cold. I feel nothing like any kind of a hero. I was a coward, I hid and I couldn't protect Grace or

Syd when I needed to. But as the ninja wraps me in a silver foil blanket I see that both Grace and Syd are looking at me through their dripping fringes as if I just single-handedly saved the day. What the fuck?

Syd

Being in the back of the car with Mum at last had been a huge relief, heading away from the centre and back towards home. They were both lost in thoughts of what they would be doing this evening, now that it was over. Syd looked at Grace and could see the sadness in her eyes. She was trying to hide it, but she knew she wasn't the only person that her Mum wanted to be with tonight. Maybe it wouldn't be over, she had thought that he had felt the same way, she would make sure that she kept nudging them in the right direction. Their earlier conversation had not deterred her from thinking she should keep trying, although Mum's response had not seemed to hold much optimism. She would drop it for now, but it wasn't like Mum to be this defeatist, she decided she would think of it as a work in progress.

She was leaning over to ask Carl to turn on the radio when the car came to a sudden screeching stop, forcing her face against the headrest of the seat in front of her. The car skidded slightly to one side before Carl corrected it and safely stopped. Then, through the rain she saw the driver of the other car - Dan? - walking towards them. She started to ask what was wrong when she saw him raise his arm and heard two muffled bangs. The car jolted slightly as Carl told them to duck down, now! A sudden realisation that they are being shot at made her stifle a scream, she ducked behind the seat and covered her mouth.

From the front of the car Carl spoke, calm and measured,

"Do what he asks, don't question it. I promise you I will do everything I can to keep you safe and help is already on the way. I can't afford for you two to get in the middle of any gunfire, but I won't let you out of my sight."

Then the front door opened and Carl was gone, leaving them alone in the car. She saw Dan walking towards them with his gun raised. He looked around then put his head through the open door.

"Where the fuck is he?"

Syd assumed this was a rhetorical question and said nothing until Dan turned to her and Grace and shouted, "Where did he fucking go?"

They both shrugged and Syd managed an answer, "I don't know, he jumped out of the car when you shot at us."

"Bollocks! I always knew he was chickenshit. Come on, get out and follow me, don't try to run or you will regret it."

They got out and walked to the front of the car.

"Now walk towards my car, stay close together and don't try anything funny."

Syd feels Grace's hand slip into her own and is glad. Whatever is going on here it's definitely not good. Where the hell is Carl when they need him? And what has happened to Mum's ex? She has to shake off a dreadful mental image of him slumped dead in the passenger seat of Dan's car. Has Carl really got them in sight? Dan has clearly had the same thought, he is scanning the pools of shadow around the car with his gun held in front of him.

They are ushered, with a point of the gun, towards the other car. Syd can see another car approaching from far off, she thinks of running and looks around at the nearby rocks, but the tremble in her legs, along with the fear of what might happen to Mum if she did try, kept her moving forward. Grace's hand tightened its grip on hers and she whispered, "It's okay, everything's going to be alright."

She doesn't know why Mum would think this, it seems very fucking not alright at the moment. Nevertheless, she found it reassuring to hear her say it, she returned the firm grip with a squeeze and grasped her hand more tightly. They arrived at the other car and were motioned to stop while Dan stepped forward to meet the approaching vehicle.

In the combined lights of the cars she saw a shadow of a figure get out of the recently arrived car. First in silhouette, then features emerging from the shadows that enveloped his face. The now familiar figure of the American started to stride towards them, grinning his gap-toothed grin, long coat darkening as the rain greeted it. Her stomach lurched, she felt sick and panic rose inside her as she realised what was happening - and that there was nothing she could do about it.

The men spoke briefly and inaudibly, then started to walk slowly towards them. Dan looked around nervously, the American kept his eyes firmly on his prize, a cold gleam in his eyes. Just as they approached there was a loud popping noise from the car behind them, another gunshot? Syd flinched before realising it had not been loud enough for that. Both men briefly turned to look in the direction of the sound.

What happened next was a blur. There was a flurry of movement from the ditch next to them and a grotesque, mud-covered figure appeared. It covered the distance in an instant, a dripping black arm flashed out as it reached Dan, who had just barely orientated his gun to be pointing in the direction of this new threat. Dan dropped his gun and collapsed to his knees clutching his throat, clearly struggling to breath. She recognised, through the layer of slime, that it was Carl, face blackened, eyes ablaze. He turned to the American, who was reaching under his coat towards his waistband and the handle of a pistol. Carl started to raise his own gun, but as he pulled it up it snagged on the flapping wet edge of his jacket. His hand, slippery with mud and rain water could not keep its grip and the gun fell to the ground with a metallic clatter.

"Fuck!"

The American now pointed his own gun towards Carl and drawled, "I think I owe you one you cocksucker. Give me a fucking reason to shoot you and I fucking will."

Carl stood facing him, calm and alert. He raised his arms, palms open and facing outward, then laced his fingers behind his head.

Rounders had been Syd's game of choice at university, mostly because she liked the informality of playing in a park with whoever decided to turn up on the day. The easy going nature of it had not made her any less competitive, the games were invariably raucous and fun. It was during these knockabout games that she had found she had an aptitude for pitching.

She slipped her hand from Grace's and reached into her bag, which she had kept on her shoulder. Her fingers closed around the can of coke she had put in earlier. The American had his eyes firmly fixed on Carl, he evidently did not perceive any threat from either of the two women, he was telling Carl to kneel slowly, watching all the time for any sudden movements.

In one swift movement she launched the tin towards the American, focusing all her anger and fury over the way her life had been turned upside down by that conniving, duplicitous bastard Rick. A combination of skill, luck and raw rage, in equal measures, saw the trajectory of the tin arch directly across the short distance. Its entire passage accompanied by a drawn-out banshee screech of the single word '**baaastaaard!**', at full volume. The American looked around as the tin went straight to the centre of his forehead. It struck him with a clearly audible clunk, followed by a brief hissing sound as it burst open and started to spray its contents into the air, spinning its way to the ground. The next few seconds seemed to happen in slow motion, an eternity of dreadful anticipation as he looked towards Syd, she saw his gun hand start to move in her direction and flinched and ducked reflexively. Then, as he started to turn towards her, his eyes rolled back up in his head and he fell backwards, landing flat on his back and staying there unmoving and limp.

Carl glanced at her, a look of surprise on his face, before quickly retrieving his own gun. He stood back up as a figure came out of the light towards them, pointing his gun in that direction briefly before lowering it, kneeling down and starting to remove Dan's boot laces. The figure, dripping mud and water, lurching slightly and wielding a vicious-looking knife in a raised and bloodied hand staggered towards them. Mum had started to run towards him before Syd even realised who it was, when the penny finally dropped she ran to join them, just as a helicopter swooped in from overhead, spraying the rain furiously around them as their would-be rescuers dropped in to find their work already done for them.

Alice

What a fuck up. She would have never believed that the Americans would try something so brazen – or stupid. Nor would she have believed that Dan would be the inside man. Now her centre was full again; she had a bunch of men in fatigues keeping Mrs B running around with trays of tea and coffee. There were two men in Alice's 'special visitors' rooms. One of them would not be going outside again for a very long time to come. The other would undoubtedly be picked up by a fellow countryman sometime soon. They would claim he was an employee at the embassy and invoke diplomatic immunity, then demand his release. He would go, of course, but he certainly wouldn't be visiting the UK again anytime soon, diplomat or not. He would also have a semi-circular bruise in the centre of his forehead for some time – a souvenir of his outing.

There were also two scared ladies, currently having hot showers and getting dry clothes, and a mud soaked man having his hand stitched back together in sick bay. This was going to take some time to sort out.

She had already sent a copy of the flash drive to her contact in Whitehall. Tomorrow morning the American ambassador would be summoned to an urgent meeting where he would be told, in no uncertain terms, that this situation was closed, unless they wanted all of this to go public. She was confident, now that both her rogue agent and their attack dog were out of the picture, that this would now be an end to the matter.

Carl was sitting in her office with her. He had stripped off his wet clothes and was wearing a pair of joggers and a clean tee shirt, his face, arms and hands were still smeared with patches of dry and flaking mud which fell in flurries when he raised his hands to drink his coffee.

"What a fuck up," she said.

"And then some," Carl agreed.

"I'm still hazy on the details, how did you take out both of them? I mean, I know you're good, that's why I got you on board – but that was a tall order even for you."

"Well, after I read the notes on our Yank friend I decided I wouldn't take any chances, I took provisions and precautions and was on the lookout for anything odd, I was worried he'd try something. Dan though, what a cunt! – excuse my language. I can't believe he shot out the car radiator and lights while they were still in it. Anyway, the truth is, Ma'am, I wasn't on my own."

He relayed the sequence of events, describing everybody else's role, the bravery and composure he had seen would have put some of his erstwhile professional colleagues to shame. He re-counted the felling of the American with a coke tin with particular relish and detail. He downplayed his own input, after all, he was only doing his job. He knew there was no way he would have salvaged things on his own.

"They are a gutsy bunch ma'am," he concluded.

"They are that. Still, gutsy or not, I want them all home. I've kept that chopper on site, let's use it and get them straight there shall we? I want some of our most reliable people watching their doors too."

"Yes, Ma'am, I'll see to it personally," replied Carl.

Alice looked at him and was glad he was on her side. She wasn't sure when he had last slept, she didn't know when he managed to eat and she was certain he hadn't had a day off in months.

"No you won't, once you've organised things, I want you to take some leave."

"But, Ma'am…"

"No, that's an order - forced R & R. You can use the company travel pass if you want to go and get some sunshine." She looked at his face and thought that was probably not what he wanted. Her best guess was that by this time tomorrow he would be half way up a mountain somewhere, each to his own eh?

"Yes, Ma'am," he stood up and put his empty mug on the table. "I'll just go and shower, then I'll get them loaded up."

"Thanks Carl." Alice watched him leave, the trail of mud flakes and dirt making her smile as she wondered what Mrs B would make of what was happening here. Alice imagined she would be as inscrutable as ever, either welcoming the excitement or decrying the mess and confusion – or both in equal measure. She did know that these recent, egregious lapses of security meant that maybe it was time to wind this centre down. It would stay operational, just not in its current capacity, she wondered what Mrs B would choose to do when that happened.

Returning to the meeting room she found her now dry and mud-free trio of guests waiting for her. One had a large bandage on his hand, all looked shell-shocked and tired.

"I won't spend time on goodbye, we did that already. We're going to get you home now, as quickly as possible. Without wanting to sound too inhospitable, please don't come back this time. I'm sorry about this afternoon but wanted to say well done to all of you, Carl tells me you all acquitted yourselves well."

She bids them farewell as a now clean Carl comes to tell them their transport is ready. He escorts them across the car park, where the rain has now become a fine misty veil that reflects the bright lights on the perimeter. It gives their hair a fresh sheen of silver droplets that both Grace and Syd shake out before getting into the waiting helicopter.

CHAPTER 19
Homecoming

Miraculously I still have my house keys. I find the correct one instinctively, put it in the lock and open the door. I have seen that my car has already been returned, it's parked outside when I arrive home –after my second ever helicopter trip. Actually, my third, but I'm a bit hazy about the details of the last one. We land once for Grace and Syd to clamber out and into a waiting car for the remainder of their journey. It's all a bit awkward – we're all tired, the adrenaline has worn off and all anybody really wants is to go to bed. We part with promises to speak soon.

I expect the flat to be musty and airless, but in reality I have only been gone for a few days. Not enough time for entropy to be evident in my house plants, although they do need some water. My belongings have also been returned, they are in a neatly packed box on the kitchen table, along with some essential food items – bread, milk and a bottle of wine. Very thoughtful.

I check my new phone, remarkably undamaged during the melee on the moors. There are very few messages, and none that I feel inclined to reply to right now. Some are from Nicole, I don't even read them, I guess I'll have to speak to her again sometime, but not now. I put the phone down on the table and inspect the rest of the flat.

It is exactly as I left it; records in their shelves, stacks of CDs next to the overflowing bookcase and its precarious piles of surplus books. Same old pictures, same old everything. It is familiar and comforting, but now it feels as if something is missing, as if it needs more somehow – although it would be hard to squeeze in any more than my twenty plus years of possessions that are currently crammed in and on the cupboards and shelves.

I am tired, my head's telling me to go to bed, but I find myself unable to as I pace restlessly around the flat before letting myself out and going for a walk along the moonlit beach. I wrap my coat around myself against the cold night air. The lapping tide somehow manages to synchronise with the throbbing in my hand as the effect of the painkillers they gave me in the medical bay begins to wear off. Ghost-like gulls glide silently above me in the starless sky and it feels good to be in a familiar place, safe and at home. But I do not feel as if it is the right place anymore, what I want most is not here.

Finally, I return, tired and ready to sleep. I drop my clothes on the chair by the bed and try to settle down, but the bed is empty and cold and my mind races through its usual round of unanswered questions. I eventually fall asleep in the early hours of the morning.

I wake late the next day and look out at blue sky and weak autumn sunshine. As far as I am aware I have nothing to do today, and all day to do it. I have a leisurely shower then choose what to wear from the full wardrobe that is finally available to me again. Faded jeans, Nirvana tee shirt and a hoodie should be warm enough for today, certainly comfortable enough.

I am now starting to wonder what I am going to tell people to explain my absence. It has only been a short time, but I did drop completely off the radar. I know at least some people will have noticed and will be curious – hopefully not Nicole. I have an explanation ready that is near to the truth; an old college friend contacted me and asked for my help. It is close enough to being true to be watertight without going into the who, what and where's? I decide to test it on my parents first and see how it goes down.

Walking up through the town I realise, maybe for the first time, that this is not the town I grew up in. The shops of my childhood have been replaced with rows of charity shops, coffee places and the same generic outlets you find in any high street in every other town–interchangeable with town centres everywhere.

I miss the second-hand book shop that used to be on the corner, at the bottom of the hill, the family bakery a few doors up and the tiny confectioners that sold every type of sweet that you ever heard of, from jars stacked from floor to ceiling on shelves that required a set of steps to be reached. I remember how, when we were kids, we used to specifically select those high-up jars, just to see the irritation of the owner as he was forced to climb the ladder.

All gone now, everything has moved on. I walk past the phone shops and takeaways until I get to the road my parents live on, a road I remember playing in as a child – ready to dodge out of the way if a car happened to come along. It is now so choked with cars that it is even hard to walk on the pavement in places.

Arriving at their house, it looks tired. I did my best over the summer, but the garden has swarmed back in the autumn warmth, the paint is faded and peeling in places – I'll need to get to that before the winter sets in. I let myself in, calling out as I step through the door. There is no reply, so I explore downstairs and find them both asleep in the conservatory, gently snoring with sections of a dismembered newspaper in their respective laps and sliding onto the floor. I leave them there and go and put the kettle on.

I am sitting at the table when Dad comes in.

"Hello, when did you get here?"

"I just got in," I lie, my tea is almost gone, "I didn't want to wake you."

"You should've done, Mum will be pleased to see you – I'll let her know you're here. Put the kettle on again would you?"

He goes to get Mum while I start clumsily making drinks for everyone with my bandaged hand. Soon we are all sat around the table with steaming mugs in front of us. There is initial consternation about my injury. I play it down, telling them it was quite a shallow cut, that I caught it on the bread knife when I was washing up. They seem satisfied with my explanation and drop it, after a stern maternal warning about being careful with the sharp knives. I am sure that they would not really want to know the actual circumstances that had caused it, would have been horrified in fact. I'll let them carry on thinking it was a kitchen related event.

I am treated to news of what has happened to whom at church this week and what they had been up to. Mostly going out for coffee and a visit to the hospital for Dad to see the physio about his wrist, which was healing up but needed some exercises – or, to be more precise, some exercises he would actually remember to do. I also get news about my brother and sister and their various assorted children; everyone is doing well apparently. Eventually the conversation turns to me.

"We haven't seen you for a couple of days, what have you been up to?"

"Oh, I went to visit Grace."

"You never said you were going."

"No, well it was kind of spur of the moment."

This seems to satisfy them, they ask about Grace and reminisce about my college days – I thought it was me that was supposed to do that – before the conversation moves on. I look at their lined faces, they both seem to have got smaller and more careful. Precise movements that remind me of birds, pecking fussily around the biscuit tin. I am thinking about this when I realise that they are both looking at me expectantly. I have missed a question. I am tired still and not thinking as clearly as I normally would, I had been trying to plan what I wanted to talk to them about, I had prepared some careful words and was going to cautiously work my way round to the topic. Now I just blurt it out, "I'm thinking of moving. Away. Nearer to Grace."

They both look at me, "About bloody time!" says Dad.

"Okay, love, do you want to stay for tea?" asks Mum.

That was it, as simple as that. I can think of nothing better right now than a home-cooked meal and I take Dad's comments as being a blessing for my venture. It is just as well, as I am sure that Alice will have already started to pull the necessary strings and make the arrangements that I asked for her help with. I sigh heavily, smile and stand up.

"Let me help, Mum. I can still do some things with my good hand."

Of course, she didn't let me. Together with Dad she bumbled around the kitchen, procuring a meal from apparently nowhere. All the while they asked questions about where I would be going and when. For a while I was sure I wouldn't be able to go through with it, but the enthusiasm in their questions and their curiosity told me it would be alright – I had their blessing.

Later I walked on the beach. Even with the misty rain swirling in my face and soaking my jeans, trying it's best to drive me back into the warmth of my flat, it felt like home. Would I miss it? Probably, yes. Would I regret moving? On balance I thought probably not. Time would tell.

Alice

After all he had been through, at her request, it was the least she could do to help organise a relocation for him, she asked Mrs B to start making the arrangements for him. With her usual efficiency she nodded, made a note in her pad and said, "Leave it with me."

Alice was confident that this was now as good as done, she would follow up of course – she owed him that. She didn't know if he would be able to see it through, but hoped he would, he had been trapped for too long.

So often she did not see how her work impacted on people, what difference she made to people's lives – for better or for worse. Watching him had been a constant reminder for her of the good that she could do, that her actions could help people to live better, safer lives. But it also helped remind her that people carry things in their mental baggage for years, long after the actual events themselves.

She sat back in her chair, looked at the myriad things waiting for her attention and sighed, letting a momentary silence engulf her. She thought about the last few years, despite everything they had been working on, it did not feel as if the world was becoming a safer or better place. If anything, it seemed more chaotic than ever: riots, re-emerging tensions in Northern Ireland, the ongoing war in Afghanistan and the turmoil in the Middle East. It all felt as if they had been running to stand still.

She knew she was tired, it had been a busy few days – but then, when wasn't it? It was definitely the right time to pass on the baton to someone with more energy and fewer years. She clicked on her screen and opened a picture of her grandparents' farm. She had been sure it would make the ideal place to retire, her recent visit reminded her how it felt to be 'at home'. She wasn't sure what she would do, but she had to acknowledge that she was just as trapped as anybody else. She clicked open an email tab and began to type a message to her superior – someone she had never met in person in all the years she had been in charge, at least not knowingly. It could, of course, be someone she had met on numerous occasions and been blissfully unaware. She understood the need for this security, but the dehumanizing aspect of her work, the secrecy and nefariousness of the job was not something she was going to miss.

CHAPTER 20
Reunion

The woods are cold, but not as cold as the trail across the top of the open field, where the wind slices keenly across the hill. It makes me pull my hat down over my ears and wrap my coat more tightly around myself. I carry on, head down, watching my muddy boots and counting down the steps back to civilisation and the warmth of indoors. It has been a glorious, bright afternoon, but now the sun is sinking rapidly, sliding down towards the horizon. What little warmth it had offered has drained away now. Reaching the paved road, I am in sight of the house and pick up my pace, eager to get back inside.
"Hold up, you're going too fast!"

"No, you're going too slow – come on, I need the loo."

"You'll have to wait for me, I've got the key."

I reach into my pockets with my gloved hands and realise she is right. Damn.

"I'll get Syd to let me in."

"You'll be lucky, if she's not asleep she'll have the music on too loud to hear you."

I admit defeat and slow my pace, letting Grace catch up with me. As she reaches me I put my arm around her and bend to kiss the small part of her face I can see between her hat and scarf. She intercepts me and rubs her nose against mine, laughing. Then we finish the short distance to the house together, arm in arm. Grace unlocks the door for me, causing the warmth of the central heating to rush out to greet us. We push into the doorway at the same time, squeezing and shoving good-naturedly.

"What happened to ladies first?"

"Cold, that's what happened. Anyway, that's for gentlemen."

"All true, but even so…"

She stops talking and stands looking at the coat pegs. I look too, but all I see is the usual array of coats, bags and scarves. No, that's not true, on the end peg is a different coat – a blue coat that I recognise instantly. Last time I saw it, it was waiting for me at the end of the beach. My heart sinks as my mind races to try and second guess why it might be here now. Grace is already on her way to the kitchen, from where the sound of laughter is emanating. I follow her.

I still have my coat on and my hat is in my hand as I walk into the back of a stationary Grace. She is looking at Syd and Alice, who are sat at the table with hot drinks in front of them enjoying something one of them has said. Syd looks over and calmly asks if we want something to warm us up as she reaches across to switch the kettle on again.

Unable to think of anything else to say I reply, "Tea please."

Grace is more composed, if a little more direct,

"What are you doing here?"

Alice answers, "It's a social visit – mostly. Take your coats off and join us."

We do as we are told and soon we are all gathered round the table with drinks in front of us.

"This is a bit compulsive isn't it?" Alice says as she picks up a fragment of a window and neatly slots it into the correct building. I have to admit that it is, I thought that I had given up doing jigsaws when I was about six or seven-years-old. This puzzle is a town on a river with a bridge. It is nearly three quarters complete.

"Anyway, how are you all? Syd tells me her studies are going well."

We catch her up with the happenings. I moved into a flat nearby – with help from Mrs Baker. It was a wrench I'll admit, leaving behind everything and everyone was scary and I'm not sure I would have gone through with it if I hadn't had someone gently pushing me along. Yes, Syd had been in touch with me regularly, checking my progress and encouraging me. She had been pestering Grace to do the same - although truth be told, once things started to happen the momentum of events took over. Grace openly admits that she did not believe I would be able to do it, and I am pathetically pleased with myself for having gone through with it. I am still visiting my parents regularly, one weekend a fortnight. To be fair, this is probably about as much as I used to see them previously anyway, and this way they have me staying in their house, so I am available to do all the odd jobs and chores that they have saved up for me. Every visit involves at least one mandatory walk along the beach.

My new flat is bare and functional, it is not really home yet, things are still in boxes and semi-unpacked. This is mainly because I haven't spent very many nights there, mostly I am here at Grace's house. We haven't talked about it specifically yet, but I think I might be formally moving in at some point, I hope so anyway. I'm not sure how I will downsize my book, CD and record collections to fit, but I'm sure we'll figure it out.

Syd has decided to stay living at home for now. She changed courses and is relishing the free board and lodgings, leaving her spare cash for taxis into town – and driving lessons – so she can keep up with her social life. One day last week she waited for Grace to go out to the shops then sat down with me, tea and a packet of biscuits.

"How long did it take for you to, you know, settle down again after?"

I thought about it, then answered,

"Not too long, but that's because your mum found me."

"Found you?"

"Her and her friend Shelly kind of adopted me."

"Shelly? Shelly from Swindon?"

"Yes, is she still in touch?" I had no idea, Grace hadn't mentioned her.

"God yes, she came to stay when dad first left. She's mad as a box of frogs. One night she got Mum drunker than I've ever seen her, then they spent the night Facebook stalking everybody Dad has ever known and leaving messages. Most of them not very nice. Dad was furious, serves him right though."

I laugh, "Same old Shelly then."

"It took Mum ages to calm Dad down, like he didn't deserve it."

"Harsh, I'm not getting involved in that conversation."

"Quite right too. Anyway, you never answered my question, how long?"

"I don't know, sometimes I forgot, other times I couldn't think about anything else. It's probably going to be better for you though. I couldn't talk to anybody about it. You've got Grace – and me if you want."

Syd didn't answer straight away, she came over and gave me a big hug. I have to admit I felt very paternal and protective when she did that, like maybe I'd missed out on something by not having children.

"I'm glad you're here, thanks for coming back. Are you going to move in properly?"

"Your mum hasn't asked me."

"Twat!," the hug ends and a punch on the arm takes its place. Now I really feel like part of the family. "Just ask, she'll say yes."

"I will," I tell her, and I mean it, "I'm just waiting for the right time."

Syd left it at that and the conversation moved on to more mundane matters.

Grace is happy, she still makes regular asides and comments about her house full of international fugitives – I think that will be ongoing. But she has been more like her old self, fun, funny, outgoing and sexy. She has told Ed we are back together, he subsequently claimed that he always knew she wanted me not him. Sounds a bit bitter to me, but I am so not getting involved in that – unless I need to leap to Grace's defence. But she can hold her own, and she has Shelly on her side, so I'm not needed in the defending scheme of things really. Shelly has threatened to visit soon, which I am looking forward to and dreading in equal measure. No, not really, I'm totally looking forward to it.

I suspect that Alice already knew most of this already, the surveillance cars are still ongoing and I've seen them following Syd to Uni on more than one occasion, even though they try to be discreet. I guess it's just a precaution now, I hope so at least. She comes to the point.

"I really popped by to say goodbye, I've decided to call it a day. I wanted to check in on you all and give you the details for your new contact, although the wrangling is finished now – nobody should be bothering you again. The team aren't standing down yet, but they will start to draw back soon. Everything should go back to normal."

"You're leaving?" I ask, latching on to the most important piece of information as always.

"Retiring actually, this job was my last."

"What are you going to do?"

"Disappear. I'll still have contacts though, if it flares up again I'll be around."

For some reason I draw a great deal of comfort from this, I can see that the others do too.

"Will we be able to visit America?" Syd asks.

"Really?" Grace looks at her, "Since when did you want to go to America?"

"I don't, it was just a hypothetical question."

Grace rolls her eyes and Alice answers.

"Probably not, I would find other parts of the world to holiday in. The Department of Homeland Security would still want to ask you a lot of questions, given half a chance."

There is a moment of silence, then Syd asks, "Is Alice your real name?"

"Yes, yes it is."

"Thank you Alice, I never had chance to say it before, but I know you did your best to keep us safe. I'm glad it was you."

Alice looks at me, then back to Syd,

"You're welcome, I know sometimes people have a poor opinion of the work we do, but for me it was always about keeping people safe. Especially people like you who ended up in situations that where not of your making, you were just in the wrong place at the wrong time."

I feel an old familiar flood of guilt, because my 'situation' had been at least partly my own doing. I also think I don't really know what the 'work' that Alice is referring to is, I've always had the general gist of it of course – undercover, spying, abducting, interrogating and incarcerating bad people. Beyond that I can't even guess at the specifics – and suspect I would still not know even if I asked directly. Maybe I don't even want to know.

"Do you want to stay for tea?" Grace asks.

"No thank you, I was actually on my way to somewhere else, I just wanted to drop in, sorry it was unannounced. I'm glad to see you're all okay."

She stands to leave and carefully places a card on the table with the name Chris on it, along with a phone number.

"Put the number in your contacts, but don't call it unless you need to – unless you want a full armoured squad to turn up at your door."

She smiles as she says the last, then winks and goes to get her coat while Syd gets the door for her.

After she has left Syd retreats to her room to study, the music filters through to the downstairs rooms – I don't mind, it's my copy of Hole's LP – Nobody's Daughter. God that girl has good taste!

"Who's going to protect me if the guards are pulling out?" Grace asks.

"Eh?"

"Who's going to…. oh never mind, are you going to move in, Rambo?"

Okay, hints I'm not good at – direct questions usually get a response.

"I'll go and start packing."

"No you won't, come here."

Grace takes my hand and leads me to the stairs.

"Syd'll hear us."

"Not with that racket on she won't."

I want to take umbrage at Grace's description of the music as racket, but decide that now isn't the time.

CHAPTER 21
Graduation

I am uncomfortable, squeezed into a suit that already feels too hot for the day. Grace looks fantastic in a blue wrap-around dress, her hair plaited back and a blue scarf draped over her shoulders. Syd is long gone, off to find her erstwhile study buddies and drinking partners. Next time we see her she will be walking onto the stage to collect her first class honours degree. I can't take any of the credit for this really, but I can join in with the celebrations and share the pride.
Of course, Grace has a different opinion. She thinks my presence has been just what Syd needed after her experience. Plus, of course, I single-handedly rescued her from the American. Well, I may let Carl and Syd take some of the credit for that, to be honest the whole situation still makes regular appearances in my dreams and nightmares. It has varying outcomes, but I rarely wake feeling heroic. Grace knows when I have had those dreams, she says I rub absently at the scars on my hand afterwards. It's probably true, but they are becoming less frequent now, at least for me. I know I sometimes hear Syd restlessly wrestling with her duvet and calling out in the night.

But today is not about that, it is graduation day. Ed is going to be here of course, there is a brittle truce between him and Grace, and Syd will deign to meet with him occasionally – although she is pretty miffed that he has insisted on bringing his 'floozy' with him today. I don't think there will ever be any love lost there. The hall is packed and, as previously stated, I am already uncomfortable.

Watching Syd cross the stage and receive her certificate, I finally realise why my own parents had been so insistent on attending my graduation ceremony, which I had been ambivalent about at the time. Her face beams as she scans the hall to locate the seats where she knows Grace and I will be sitting. There is a flicker of eye contact to go with the smile then she hesitates mid-step, a pause that is barely there – but I notice it.

The rest of the event drags by and I am glad to finally be released, herded out with the other relatives in a well-choreographed movement of people, all impatient to be reunited with their offspring. The tortuous trail to the designated meeting place is crowded, we jostle and push politely along with the flood of other parents until, eventually we arrive at the plaza in front of the building where we will find Syd.

Grace suggests we split up and meet at the foot of a sculpture – a swirl of twisted chrome and granite - on the far side of the crowded space, to give us a better chance of finding Syd in the crush. I agree and set off to the left, weaving through the throng. I see Syd from a distance, I would recognise her anywhere. I feel like one of those penguins that can locate a single chick amongst a gaggle of hundreds of near-identical baby penguins. Pleased with myself I make my way through the now-thinning crowd towards her, she is standing near the corner of a building talking to someone. The other person is partially obscured by the building, I catch a glimpse of a long grey/blonde plait and a pair of blue trousers disappearing as Syd turns back and starts to scan the milling group for me or Grace. I retrieve her and together we go and find Grace by the sculpture.

Syd

She hadn't really wanted to do this, parading on a stage in a bloody ridiculous gown and hat. But now the moment had arrived she felt incredibly proud, and pleased that the people she loved the most were there to witness it – even grudgingly acknowledging to herself that she was glad Dad had come. She sat amongst her peers and professors waiting for her name to be called, hoping it wouldn't take too long for this to be over. She had planned to meet up with some friends later, who would be politely saying goodbye to their own parents before meeting up for the 'proper' celebration.

Some of them would be staying at her house when they eventually rolled drunkenly in after they had trawled the pubs, clubs and bars of town. Mum had arranged to be out of the way for the night, insisting that she really wanted to spend the night in a fancy hotel, so Syd and her friends would have the house to themselves – which meant that the drinking would probably continue until whatever time they exhausted their supply of alcohol.

Her name was called and she was ushered onto the stage from where she had been waiting in the wings. As she crossed she peered into the bright lights looking for Mum, knowing roughly where she would be from the seat booking. She was glad when she saw her, reassured that this charade had not all been for nothing. But as she collected her scroll and started to walk away her eye was caught by a figure standing near one of the exits, she would recognise that face anywhere, from any distance, in any situation. What the fuck was Alice doing at her graduation? She faltered momentarily before continuing to be ushered off and out on the far side of the stage.

She got out to the front of the building as quickly as she could and made her way to the exit she thought Alice was most likely to use, pushing her way through the throng of human traffic. It was either a good guess or just lucky. Alice was there, standing near a gap between two of the buildings surrounding the open space where everyone else was congregating. Cameras were flashing and recording the day, accompanied by shrieks and hugs as friends reunited and parents were introduced then quickly dismissed. She appeared to have been looking out for Syd, expecting her, and smiled as she approached.

"I knew you'd find me."

"What are you doing here? I thought you weren't watching us anymore."

"I'm not, I came to see you graduate -congratulations."

"Why?"

"I saw your mum graduate too, just habit I guess." She smiled and Syd relaxed a bit.

"Sorry, I was just surprised, you know how it is?"

"I do indeed. Although, I wasn't entirely truthful. I am also being a postman."

"A postman?"

"Yes." She handed a plain white envelope to Syd who took it and looked at it quizzically.

"What is it?"

"Well, even though I'm retired I can still make recommendations to the service. I thought you would be a good fit, you're intelligent, resourceful, brave - and a good shot with a fizzy drink can."

"You want me to be a spy?"

"Not exactly, it's an offer to go into the pool of potential recruits. It's a very shallow pool and most people recommend family members and their friend's children – mostly public school boys if I'm honest. They need you, but it's completely up to you whether you want to open the envelope or not, there's absolutely no obligation."

"Would you do it?"

"If I could do it all over again I wouldn't hesitate. But that's just me, I can't decide for you. You can hold onto that letter, there's no time limit, or you can burn it. It's completely up to you, no pressure."

As Alice turned to leave Syd slipped the envelope into her pocket,

"Thank you."

"You're welcome."

Then Alice was gone, replaced by Mum's boyfriend who guided her towards Mum, waiting by the sculpture. Syd knew exactly what she was going to do with the envelope. If it meant she could help get bastards like Rick put away, she was up for it.

CHAPTER 22
Surprise

Alice has come to visit. It's the first time we've seen her since she told us she was retiring. This time the visit is neither unannounced nor unexpected. She rang us the evening before, told us she would be in the area, and asked if it would be okay to drop in – like normal people do. She is dressed casually, jeans, trainers, a blue and white striped top and her hair tied loosely back. She still looks great. She has a hard to qualify aura about her that makes her appear relaxed – maybe it's the easy smile or the comfortable way she carries herself.

She has apologised, unnecessarily, for intruding on our Sunday. She is now sitting comfortably on the sofa with a mug of tea in her hands, chatting with Grace. She is telling her about the different projects she has been working on over the last year, apparently pottery has become a big part of her life now. I am listening from the kitchen.

"I've been renovating the farm, I've turned one of the outbuildings into a pottery studio. You should come and visit sometime, I'm setting up a little guest cottage in the old barn. The builders tell me it will be finished before Christmas – I'll believe it when I see it."

"Are we allowed to visit, you know, with us being ...you know?" asks Grace.

"We're all civilians now, I'd like you to – if you wanted."

"As long as it's not as stressful as last time we were there," says Grace, with a smile.

"I promise, no need for Carl this time."

They laugh together at this. I think the change in Alice is not just her appearance or her posture, she seems genuinely happy now. I finally finish what I'm doing and go back to join them again.

It's not just Alice who has had a lot of change since we last met. After Syd graduated she went off travelling – not to America of course, she got a list of places she could safely go to from Alice's replacement, Chris. She spent some time with Grace's brother, her uncle, in New Zealand before launching herself onto the rest of the world. She is due back in a week or two (or 13 days if you want to be as precise as Grace) it will be good to see her again before she starts her new job.

She guilt-tripped her dad for a large part of the money to pay for this, on the promise she would pay it back when she started work. She is taking a post with the civil service, she is a little hazy on the details, and will be moving to London shortly after she returns from her wanderings. I was unaware that the government had much need for art history graduates, nevertheless that's what she's doing.

This is good for us, if a little sad for Grace, as it is giving us time and space to remember what it was like to be 'us' and get used to each other's annoying habits again. Or at least, that was the theory.

I was settling into my new job. Grace was trying to rearrange her life, house and habits to accommodate me – as well as working full-time, when she got ill. At first she thought she had picked up a bug at school, not uncommon for those of us who work with small children. I waited anxiously to see if I would succumb to it, I hate throwing up so I had been keeping my distance – while still trying to be compassionate and caring of course. The two things aren't really mutually compatible, and it had gone on for over a week. So I was keeping out of the way in the loft, sorting through my boxes of surplus possessions that had been there since I moved in, when Grace shouted up the ladder.

"Can you do something for me?"

"What's that?" I asked showing my head through the hatch, "I didn't catch it."

"I want you to do something for me."

"Anything for you my lovely – as long as it's not holding your hair back again."

"Stupid. No, I want you to go and get something."

"Where from?" I ask as I descend.

"The chemist."

"Okay," I am facing her now, "something for your stomach?"

"Not exactly." She looked at me and I could see real worry on her face, she took my hand.

"You've heard of suppressed memories right?"

I was confused now, not sure where this was going.

"Sure, when something bad happens and your brain shuts it away in a locked box in the back of your memory room – I know all about them. Why?"

"Well, I've just remembered when I was sick like this before."

She looked at me expectantly, but I didn't know what I was supposed to infer from this information. Grace elaborated.

"It was before I had Syd….about nine months before."

There was a silent pause that seemed to stretch out interminably, then I got it.

"Do you think….? I mean are you?"

"I don't know, that's why I want you to go to the chemist and get a test."

"But I thought…."

"Yeah, me too. My periods had all but petered out, the doctor said he thought it was probably the start of an early menopause. I thought I was finished with babies."

I'll admit I didn't know what to say, do, or think at that particular moment in time – it was all new territory for me - apart from the time an ex-girlfriend had told me her period was a week late. I had spent the next four or five days thinking about cots, nappies and a bigger flat before she told me that it was okay. She had found out the day after she told me but had 'forgotten to mention it'.

Finally I figure out what I'm supposed to do, I step forward and take Grace in my arms, hold her tight and say, "I'll go now, are you okay?"

"I'm worried that this isn't what you want."

"I hadn't even thought about it until thirty seconds ago, if you are pregnant it will be fantastic, we'll be a great mum and dad."

"You're not going to leave me then?"

"God no! It's taken me twenty five years to find you again, I'm not going to let you go that easily – I love you."

And I mean it, I kiss her then go downstairs and get my car keys and wallet.

Later we are sitting looking at the blue line together.

"Are you sure?"

I have had a little time to process this now, It's a surprise – but a good surprise. Until this afternoon I hadn't even realised how much I wanted this, I guess spending time around Syd had made me realise what I'd missed out on by not being a dad.

"I've never been more sure about anything. Are you?"

"I'm worried, I'll be old for a mum."

"You're not old." I pause for a moment then continue, "God, we'll be retired by the time it goes to university."

"I am old, but I'm happy. Let's do it!"

There were lots of appointments, the doctors like to closely monitor what they, rather charmlessly, call 'geriatric pregnancies', the cheek of it. They were most insistent that Grace should have an amnio synthesis, Grace declined because of the potential risk to the baby. I didn't contradict her, it's her body. Syd was delighted, promising to take a break from her voyages when the baby was born. She was good to her word, making a special round trip from Madrid to meet her new brother when he finally made his grand entrance.

Once the sickness had subsided it was just a question of watching Grace get bigger, making sure she was comfortable, massaging her feet and stomach with cocoa butter and getting the spare room set up as a nursery – losing my records to the loft again.

I was, and still am, excited. Grace has done this before, but it is a new adventure for me. Every kick gave me butterflies and Grace indigestion, I wanted it to last forever, and to be over. It felt like it was the thing we needed to seal the deal so to speak.

I could tell you about the birth in some considerable detail, how scared I was, how Grace gripped my hand so hard it left bruises, how I had to sit down and wait for the nurse to get me a glass of water before I was entrusted with actually holding my son for the first time. I could, but I won't, because those are things that mean everything to me and Grace but would just be another 'new dad baby birth story' to anyone else.

And now it is almost literally my whole life. I have taken a break from teaching to be a stay-at-home dad, I'm loving it. I can hardly believe that I've left it until this late in my life to do this. Actually, I know why I didn't do this before, it was because the person I was meant to share my life with wasn't available. It has completed our reunification, we are figuring things out together and it's working.

Now I have finished changing the nappy he is fit to be presented to Alice, I hold him in front of my face and look into his beautiful eyes. If you had told me last year that someone else would be taking my attention from Grace I would have poo-pooed the very idea. It's okay though, she understands.

"Who's my little man then eh? Come on, time to meet Auntie Alice."

She takes him enthusiastically but inexpertly. She coos and fusses in a way that I would never have imagined would be in her repertoire of interactions. He looks back and smiles, his blue and green eyes (one of each) locking with hers as he coos back around the tip of his tongue that protrudes slightly from his mouth.

"He's beautiful," she says, holding him in the crook of her arm and letting him grasp the fingers of her free hand. She's right, he's the most precious thing I have ever seen – although I am biased.

So, this is us – sitting together sharing smiles and tea while our world revolves around a tiny, helpless being that I am partially responsible for keeping alive – no pressure there then. Honestly, I wouldn't have it any other way. Grace beams, Alice does that baby-talk thing that people do, and I sip my tea and watch contentedly as I finally get my life as a grown up together.

Syd

It had only just begun and the lies, deceit and subterfuge was already starting. To be fair, it wasn't all untrue, she had been to visit her uncle and had spent some time travelling around the two islands. It had been fantastic, driving around in brightly painted buses with groups of backpackers and trying her hand at a variety of new activities that she hadn't even realised that she wanted to have a go at: bungee jumping, parachuting, white water rafting and even skiing. She had also seen whales and dolphins, walked on deserted beaches and had a fling with another backpacker, a tall blond Australian lad called James. This last had been the most nerve wracking for her, it was the first attempt at a relationship since her disastrous affair with Rick. But it had been a fun week and they had both promised to stay in touch after their itineraries took them off in different directions. She knew that they probably wouldn't, and that was okay with her, they'd had a fun time and it was good to be able to leave it like that.

It was after she had said goodbye to her uncle and his family at the airport that her trip had deviated from the one that everyone else thought she taking. The next 28 hours were spent in cramped discomfort on a Quantas plane, reading and watching films in between perfunctory airline meals and wedging herself against the window under a blanket and attempting to sleep. Now she looked out of the window and saw the sun rising in a golden haze as the plane came in to land at Larnaca airport, safely delivering to Cyprus. This was not Thailand, which her friends and family believed was her destination, mainly because that was what she had told them.

She hoped she'd made the right decision, but as with all things she wouldn't be certain until she had given it a try. She had opened Alice's letter and followed the directions inside, which had led to an official invitation to an interview in London. It had been weird, none of the questions seemed to have any bearing on the job that she thought she had been put forward for by Alice. Nevertheless, the interviewer seemed more than happy with the answers she gave. She put it to the back of her mind as she planned her trip to New Zealand until she got the e-mail. It told her that her travel plans had been changed and included the tickets she needed to get to the Mediterranean after she had visited her uncle and his family. It was quite explicit that she shouldn't let anybody else know about this change of plan.

Inside the airport she followed the route from the plane to immigration with the other passengers, jostling along like herded cattle through the brightly lit corridors that snaked towards the exit. She joined the end of the long queue at passport control, looking at the long line snaking between a zig-zag of movable barriers she sighed and started rummaging in her hand luggage, looking for her documents. She jumped slightly when she felt a hand on her elbow. Looking round she saw a customs official who politely asked her name, once she had confirmed who she was he asked her to follow him to a recessed door which he gestured for her to enter. It opened into a quiet side room, away from the noise and bustle of the main area.

The room was bare of all furniture apart from a desk and two chairs, black vinyl flooring and plain white walls and ceilings. There was a burst of colour in the middle of the room, sitting on the edge of the desk, wearing a brightly patterned shirt and dark chinos, and smiling from ear to ear, was a familiar face.

"Hi Syd, how was your flight?"

The flight had been long, she was tired and apprehensive about what she was embarking on. This was all forgotten once she saw Carl, she took three steps to cross the room and wrapped her arms around him.

"It was fine, I'm so glad to see you again, how are you? And what are you doing here?"

"I'm all good," he answered while disentangling himself, "I'll explain why I'm here later, are you all set?"

"I still need to go through passport control and collect my luggage."

Carl grinned, "Someone will collect your luggage for you, there's no need for passport control here – not for us anyway. It's okay, you'll get used to it."

He led her to a second door on the far side of the room and into the hidden areas of the airport that most travellers never see, empty breeze block corridors with silver pipes and conduits running along the ceiling. Eventually they came to a heavy door which led out into the bright sunshine that was rapidly warming as the day began.

"So come on then, why are you here?" Syd asked once they were in the car and navigating the busy traffic leading away from the airport.

"I asked to be. Alice told me she'd put your name forward, when Chris told me you'd actually applied I volunteered to be your mentor."

"Eh? Why?"

"Don't sound so surprised, I know what you can do with a Coke can remember. Seriously, I didn't want one of the others giving you a hard time and putting you off."

"Seriously?"

"Yeah, it's a bit of a boy's club sometimes. I'm glad you decided to join us, maybe you'll be the next Alice eh? A bit of a way to go before that though, and it all starts here. This bit of the training is quite intense, but I'm sure you'll be fine. We'll be working alongside some of the army units based here, and you'll be training for various combat and conflict situations."

They continued their drive along the long, dusty road. Carl chatted amicably about some of the things they would be covering and asked questions about her trip. Syd answered him, twisting her hair and drilling for more information about her itinerary, all the time her head swirled with the enormity of what she was embarking on. There was an element of nervousness, along with some unease. But mostly, she had to admit to herself, what she was feeling was excitement.

Steve Beed was born in 1964, since then he has seen men walking on the moon, been chased by a wild elephant and been on the TV – which makes it sound all much more exciting than it actually was. He has a beautiful wife and three grown up children and has been a teacher since finishing college in 1987.

You can write and tell me how much you liked this book at:
stevebeed64@gmail.com
In return I will let you know about new books that are in the offing.

You can follow my blog at:
https://steevbeed.wordpress.com

Printed in Great Britain
by Amazon